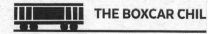 **THE BOXCAR CHILDREN MYSTERIES**

D0069066

THE MYSTERY OF THE WILD PONIES
THE MYSTERY IN THE COMPUTER GAME
THE HONEYBEE MYSTERY
THE MYSTERY AT THE CROOKED HOUSE
THE HOCKEY MYSTERY
THE MYSTERY OF THE MIDNIGHT DOG
THE MYSTERY OF THE SCREECH OWL
THE SUMMER CAMP MYSTERY
THE COPYCAT MYSTERY
THE HAUNTED CLOCK TOWER MYSTERY
THE MYSTERY OF THE TIGER'S EYE
THE DISAPPEARING STAIRCASE MYSTERY
THE MYSTERY ON BLIZZARD MOUNTAIN
THE MYSTERY OF THE SPIDER'S CLUE
THE CANDY FACTORY MYSTERY
THE MYSTERY OF THE MUMMY'S CURSE
THE MYSTERY OF THE STAR RUBY
THE STUFFED BEAR MYSTERY
THE MYSTERY OF ALLIGATOR SWAMP
THE MYSTERY AT SKELETON POINT
THE TATTLETALE MYSTERY
THE COMIC BOOK MYSTERY
THE GREAT SHARK MYSTERY
THE ICE CREAM MYSTERY
THE MIDNIGHT MYSTERY
THE MYSTERY IN THE FORTUNE COOKIE
THE BLACK WIDOW SPIDER MYSTERY
THE RADIO MYSTERY
THE MYSTERY OF THE RUNAWAY GHOST
THE FINDERS KEEPERS MYSTERY
THE MYSTERY OF THE HAUNTED BOXCAR
THE CLUE IN THE CORN MAZE
THE GHOST OF THE CHATTERING BONES
THE SWORD OF THE SILVER KNIGHT
THE GAME STORE MYSTERY
THE MYSTERY OF THE ORPHAN TRAIN
THE VANISHING PASSENGER
THE GIANT YO-YO MYSTERY
THE CREATURE IN OGOPOGO LAKE
THE ROCK 'N' ROLL MYSTERY
THE SECRET OF THE MASK
THE SEATTLE PUZZLE
THE GHOST IN THE FIRST ROW
THE BOX THAT WATCH FOUND
A HORSE NAMED DRAGON

THE GREAT DETECTIVE RACE
THE GHOST AT THE DRIVE-IN MOVIE
THE MYSTERY OF THE TRAVELING TOMATOES
THE SPY GAME
THE DOG-GONE MYSTERY
THE VAMPIRE MYSTERY
SUPERSTAR WATCH
THE SPY IN THE BLEACHERS
THE AMAZING MYSTERY SHOW
THE PUMPKIN HEAD MYSTERY
THE CUPCAKE CAPER
THE CLUE IN THE RECYCLING BIN
MONKEY TROUBLE
THE ZOMBIE PROJECT
THE GREAT TURKEY HEIST
THE GARDEN THIEF
THE BOARDWALK MYSTERY
THE MYSTERY OF THE FALLEN TREASURE
THE RETURN OF THE GRAVEYARD GHOST
THE MYSTERY OF THE STOLEN SNOWBOARD
THE MYSTERY OF THE WILD WEST BANDIT
THE MYSTERY OF THE SOCCER SNITCH
THE MYSTERY OF THE GRINNING GARGOYLE
THE MYSTERY OF THE MISSING POP IDOL
THE MYSTERY OF THE STOLEN DINOSAUR BONES
THE MYSTERY AT THE CALGARY STAMPEDE
THE SLEEPY HOLLOW MYSTERY
THE LEGEND OF THE IRISH CASTLE
THE CELEBRITY CAT CAPER
HIDDEN IN THE HAUNTED SCHOOL
THE ELECTION DAY DILEMMA
JOURNEY ON A RUNAWAY TRAIN
THE CLUE IN THE PAPYRUS SCROLL
THE DETOUR OF THE ELEPHANTS
THE SHACKLETON SABOTAGE
THE KHIPU AND THE FINAL KEY
THE DOUGHNUT WHODUNIT
THE ROBOT RANSOM
NEW! THE LEGEND OF THE HOWLING WEREWOLF
NEW! THE DAY OF THE DEAD MYSTERY

3 1526 05177693 5

THE BOXCAR CHILDREN®

CREATED BY
GERTRUDE CHANDLER WARNER

INTERACTIVE MYSTERY

MIDNIGHT AT THE HAUNTED HOTEL

STORY BY JM LEE

ILLUSTRATED BY HOLLIE HIBBERT

ALBERT WHITMAN & COMPANY
CHICAGO, ILLINOIS

Copyright © 2018 by Albert Whitman & Company

First published in the United States of America
in 2018 by Albert Whitman & Company

ISBN 978-0-8075-2850-1

All rights reserved. No part of this book may be reproduced or transmitted in any
form or by any means, electronic or mechanical, including photocopying,
recording, or by any information storage and retrieval system,
without permission in writing from the publisher.

THE BOXCAR CHILDREN® is a registered
trademark of Albert Whitman & Company.

Printed in the United States of America
10 9 8 7 6 5 4 3 2 1 LB 22 21 20 19 18

Illustrations by Hollie Hibbert

Visit the Boxcar Children online at www.boxcarchildren.com.
For more information about Albert Whitman & Company,
visit our website at www.albertwhitman.com.

MIDNIGHT AT THE HAUNTED HOTEL

CHOOSE A PATH.
FOLLOW THE CLUES.
SOLVE THE MYSTERY!

Can you help the Boxcar Children crack the case? Follow the directions at the end of each section to decide what the Aldens do next. But beware—some routes will end the story before the case is solved. After you finish one path, go back and follow the other paths to see how it all turns out!

ARRIVAL

"There it is, up on the hill," said Grandfather.

Violet looked out the window as the Aldens' car exited a grove of old oak trees. The mansion was still far off, but without trees in the way, she could already see it clearly.

"It's huge!" said Benny, Violet's six-year-old brother. He leaned past her and stuck his nose up to the window to get a better view.

Jessie scooted across the back seat to get a glimpse too. She was twelve—two years older than Violet. She held a bright yellow flier, which had the words GARDNER HOTEL GRAND REOPENING at the top. Tonight was the party to celebrate the grand reopening of the old hotel. And they were helping Grandfather's friend prepare.

Fourteen-year-old Henry, the oldest, sat in the passenger's seat. He had a map open in his lap.

"Turn left up ahead, Grandfather," he said.

Grandfather turned where Henry told him to. The car moved slowly down a gravel driveway, then it pulled into a loop in front of the hotel.

"It's so old and fancy," Violet said after they were all out of the car.

Jessie nodded. "Look at those bricks. They must be over a hundred years old!"

The hotel was three stories high, all built in deep red bricks. But it's steep, pointed gables made it look much bigger and fancier. Trimmed hedges and big pots of flowers surrounded the entrance.

"Juliette sure has done a good job fixing up this place," said Grandfather. "And here she comes now!"

A woman with straight black hair walked quickly out of the hotel. She wore a rose-colored suit that matched the building. In one hand she held a clipboard, and in the other she had a cell phone.

"She looks busy," Benny whispered.

"Grand openings are busy days," said Jessie.

"Hello, James! These must be your grandchildren!" The woman put her phone in her pocket and trotted down the front steps to greet them.

"Yes," said Grandfather. "Juliette, I'd like you to meet Henry, Jessie, Violet, and Benny. Children, this is Juliette Baker, a dear old friend of mine. She bought the Gardner Hotel after it closed and has been fixing it up ever since."

Juliette shook their hands one at a time.

"Nice to meet you," Henry said. "We're looking forward to helping you get ready for the big night."

"Grandfather's told us all about the building," Jessie added, holding up the flier. "I can't believe it was closed. It's so exciting that it's reopening!"

"It's been a lot of work," said Juliette. "I'm happy for the help tonight."

"Well, you children have a lot of fun ahead of you," Grandfather said. "I'm going to go pick up supplies for the party. I'll be back in time to celebrate though."

"Thanks, Grandfather!" Henry said. "See you soon!"

They waved to Grandfather as he got in the car

and drove off. Then Juliette led the children inside.

"I'll give you a tour!" she said. "The hotel was a mansion when it was first built in the 1880s. This was what's called a grand entryway. In 1955, the Gardner family changed the mansion into a hotel, so this became the lobby. Pretty fancy, isn't it?" She winked.

"It's beautiful," said Violet.

The floor was tiled black and white, and the room was furnished with a large clock, a fireplace, and red velvet chairs and couches. Even the front desk was fancy, made of dark shiny wood carved in complex swirls.

Employees were hurrying back and forth hanging streamers and balloons and a sign that said GRAND OPENING. Two curving stairways on either side of the room led to the second floor. And in the middle was the strangest and most impressive part of the room. Between the two stairways was a shiny pipe organ.

Violet had seen pipe organs like it in books. The instrument looked like an upright piano except it had rows of brass pipes that rose out of the top.

Some of them almost reached the ceiling.

"Is that a real organ?" Violet asked.

"Yes," said Juliette. For the first time, the children saw her smile fade a little. "Let's go down to the main office. We can go over the list of things I need help with."

"Isn't the organ supposed to have a keyboard?" asked Jessie.

"Yes, but it's been missing for some time," Juliette replied quickly. It seemed like she didn't want to talk about it. "Come on. The office is this way."

As the children followed Juliette, they passed an empty hallway, and Violet thought she heard the creaking of a door. But when she looked, there was no movement. The old hallway was spooky. She reminded herself of the first day she and her siblings had come to live with Grandfather. After their parents had died, they had been living in an old boxcar in the woods. Moving from the boxcar into Grandfather's house had been a big change, and sometimes the parts of the house they hadn't explored seemed scary. But after living there and getting used to it, the kids weren't nervous about any part of the old house. Not even down in the basement where Grandfather kept his old fishing rods and garden equipment.

Juliette opened the office door and let them in. The room was like every other part of the hotel, with fancy red carpet and luxurious furniture. A man dressed in jeans and a suit coat was sitting on the couch along with a suitcase and duffel bag. He was wearing expensive, shiny shoes and had thick black eyebrows. Juliette was surprised to see him.

"Excuse me," she said. "Can I help you?"

"I'd like to book a room," the man said. "It's opening night, isn't it? The name's Eddie. Eddie Gardner."

Juliette frowned. "Eddie...Charles Gardner's son?"

The Aldens stared at Eddie. This was the son of the man who had once owned the hotel!

"Yes," said Eddie, looking serious. "But now I'm just a guest. I came to see you because the clerk said you don't allow pets. Is that true?"

"Yes. That's always been the policy in the hotels I've managed," said Juliette.

Eddie stood up and gently lifted his duffel bag.

He shook his head. "My father loved pets. He would have allowed them."

"Even so, my rule is that we don't," Juliette said. "You're welcome to stay the night if you would like. But please, it's very important that the opening goes smoothly—especially with the rumors that caused the hotel to close in the first place.

"As you may know, the historical committee is coming to see the building. If they approve the hotel as a historical landmark, it will be protected by the historical registry. Wouldn't you like to see that, for your father's sake?"

Eddie eased the duffel strap over his shoulder.

"Yes, of course I would," he said. "Even if the only reason you want it is because it would be good for business." He got up to leave the office without saying hello or good-bye to the Aldens. As he walked through the door, something caught Violet's eye. She tugged on Henry's sleeve and nodded with her chin.

"What is it?" Henry asked.

"His bag," Violet said. "I think I saw it *move!*"

CONTINUE TO PAGE 9

A MYSTERY AND A MISSION

The Aldens gathered around Juliette's desk. She shook her head.

"Having the last owner's son around is the last thing I need tonight...but I guess it can't be helped. I just hope he doesn't cause a scene. I imagine he's upset that I took over the hotel that was in his family for generations."

Jessie remembered something Juliette had said. "You mentioned rumors to Mr. Gardner. Did something happen that caused the hotel to close?" she asked.

"Well..." Juliette cleared her throat. "I might as well tell you. There are many reasons the hotel closed. I believe it's mostly because the old owner, Charles Gardner, stopped taking care of it. But many people believe that the real reason the hotel closed is because it's...haunted."

"Haunted!" cried Benny. "Like by ghosts?" He tried to imagine what it might be like to stay in a hotel haunted by ghosts. There were so many dark hallways and empty rooms. He shivered, but it was exciting to think about.

"Yes," said Juliette. "The rumors really got out of hand when Charles Gardner was running the hotel in his old age. But they're just rumors. I've never heard any of the noises or seen any ghosts. All I know is that the stories are bad for business. People don't want to stay in a hotel that might be haunted."

"Don't worry," said Jessie. She knew Juliette was worried about the opening, especially because the historical committee was going to be there. "Everything is going to go great."

Henry agreed. "Jessie's right. We're here to help you get ready. Let us know where we should start."

Juliette let out a big breath. "Right! Right. Where was that list...ah, here we go." She gave the Aldens a checklist from her clipboard. "These are the things you could help me with. When you are done, you can visit the kitchen for a snack. I let the chef know you're helping."

Jessie read over the list and handed it to Violet and Benny. Benny was just learning to read, so Violet helped him sound out some of the words.

"'Sweep the lobby. Wash the windows. Polish the railings,'" he read out loud. He knew how to do all of the things on the list! "And then the best part—snacks!"

Juliette smiled and led them out of the office. "Thank you! I'll show you where the cleaning closet is, where we keep the supplies."

As they headed toward the lobby, a man in a clerk's uniform hurried over. Jessie remembered seeing him decorating the lobby. He was out of breath. His cheeks were pale, like he'd seen something frightening. In his hand he had a white piece of paper.

"What's wrong, Alex?" asked Juliette. "You look like you've seen a ghost. Were they hoping to rent a room tonight?" She winked at Benny.

"I got a strange message just now. Someone left it at the front desk. It's...it's..." Alex had trouble finishing his sentence, so Juliette gestured for him to give her the paper. When he did, she read it out loud.

"'Bring my keys to Room 222 by midnight, or I will not rest until everyone is gone,'" she read. "What does that mean? Who left this?"

"I don't know," said Alex. "I went to help hang one of the streamers, and when I went back to the desk, it was waiting there. What keys do you think they're talking about? And isn't Room 222 off-limits?"

Juliette chewed on her lip, reading the note again. "Yes. That room isn't a guest room. No one should be staying there. Thank you, Alex. I'll take this from here, but if you see anyone suspicious, please let me know right away."

"Do you think this has something to do with... the ghost?" asked Alex.

Juliette sighed and shook her head.

"No, Alex," she said. "For the last time, there's no such thing as ghosts."

Alex looked at the Aldens with nervous eyes then nodded and hurried back to the desk.

"Who do you think could have left the message, Juliette?" Henry asked.

"Why would someone want a pair of keys?" asked Jessie. The Alden children loved solving mysteries. They knew just the right questions to ask.

Juliette tapped a finger on her chin. "When I bought the mansion, I changed the locks to all the doors," she said. "But when I did, I found there were two identical keys that didn't go to any doors in the hotel. I thought they might be important, so I kept them."

Juliette took a key ring from her pocket. Most of the keys looked new. But two of them were bigger and heavier with fancy designs on the ends. She let Benny hold the keys.

"I wonder who wants them, and why?" Juliette wondered out loud.

"Maybe they're ghost keys that can open any door!" said Benny.

"I've got an idea," said Violet. "We're going to be tidying up all over the hotel, right? How about we take the keys with us and find where they go?"

"And we'll keep our eyes open for anyone who

might have written the message," Jessie added.

"That's a great idea!" said Juliette. She took the two old keys off the ring and handed one to Henry and one to Jessie. "If we can figure out where the keys go, maybe we can figure out who wrote the message and what they want."

Henry nodded and put the key in his pocket.

"We'll take care of it," he said.

"Thank you," said Juliette. "Now, I've got to go help the chef. Please ask Alex if you need anything."

Juliette waved good-bye as she headed away.

"Where should we start?" Henry asked.

"Does anyone else want to hear the ghost story?" asked Benny. "It sounds like Alex knows it."

"You know, oftentimes ghost stories are based in truth," said Jessie. "If there's a rumor about the mansion that has to do with keys, maybe it could give us some clues about these real keys Juliette gave us."

"Let's see if he will tell us what he knows," Henry said.

They found Alex at the front desk. He was still pale from the mystery message.

"Hi, Alex," Jessie said. "Say, we heard you

mention to Juliette something about a ghost..."

"I want to hear the whole story!" Benny interrupted.

"Oh, that?" said Alex. He looked around nervously. "All right, but keep your voices down. Juliette doesn't like us talking about the ghost where guests might hear us."

Alex leaned in, and the Aldens did the same. Benny grinned with glee, waiting for Alex to speak.

"A long time ago," Alex began, "the Gardner Hotel was a mansion owned by the Gardner family. But the family fell on hard times, and they decided to turn their home into a hotel. The story goes that the boy who lived in the mansion was very upset about this. He loved to play his pipe organ. But with guests around all the time, he couldn't practice. The pipe organ was in the lobby, after all. Before long, he disappeared. No one saw him again."

"What happened to him?" asked Violet.

"The story goes that he died at a young age and that he was always mad about what happened to his home," said Alex. "Now he haunts the hotel, wandering up and down the halls and jingling his keys to remind everyone that they're in his house. And sometimes, in the middle of the night, he plays Charles Ivy pieces on the organ just to wake up the guests. Well...that's what people say, anyway. They call him the Lost Composer."

A chill raced up Benny's neck. "Wow!"

"Charles Ivy?" Violet asked. "The famous composer? I think I've heard some of his music when we've gone to see the orchestra with Grandfather."

Alex shrugged. "Yeah. Apparently whenever the organ plays, it plays Charles Ivy's music. But I wouldn't know. It stopped before Juliette bought the building."

"That's a great story," Benny said. "I wonder why Juliette doesn't want people to know about it."

"Yeah, I'd think a ghost story like that might make people more interested in visiting," Henry said.

Alex shook his head. "Not these kinds of stories. People from all over started reporting knocking noises, heavy footsteps, and jangling in the hallways. But when they looked to see what was making all the noise, there was no one there. Just shadows and sometimes ghostly shapes in the mirrors. On top of that, after guests would leave, they would find that some of their belongings were missing. Keys, wallets, jewelry, things like that. But when they called the hotel, no one would be able to find the missing objects. It's one of the reasons the hotel had to close."

When Alex was done speaking, the children stood up straight again.

"I think this will give us something to think about," said Jessie. "But what exactly, I don't know."

"Thanks for the story," said Henry. "We're going to go looking for any old locks that might fit these keys Juliette gave us. Hopefully it will help us track down whoever wrote that message."

"I just hope the Lost Composer didn't write it," said Alex.

The Aldens went to the cleaning closet to get their supplies. Henry handed Jessie a broom and took out a vacuum cleaner for himself.

"All right, let's split into two teams," he said. "Violet, how about you and I clean the lobby."

Violet nodded. "Sure. Then we can search the

first floor and the lower level to see if we can find what these keys unlock. Maybe there's something in the basement! That's where Grandfather keeps all the stuff he's forgotten about at his house, at least."

Jessie chuckled. "Benny and I will polish the bannisters and check the rooms on the upper floors," she said.

"Yeah!" Benny cheered. Getting ready for a party was fun, but it was even better now that there was a mystery to solve. "The Lost Composer isn't going to frighten any guests tonight—not if we can help it!" he said.

TO FOLLOW JESSIE AND BENNY UPSTAIRS, GO TO PAGE 19.

TO FOLLOW HENRY AND VIOLET TO THE BASEMENT, GO TO PAGE 42.

INVESTIGATING UPSTAIRS

Jessie and Benny took a few cleaning cloths, a broom, and a dustpan, and headed up the grand staircase in the lobby. Jessie started sweeping the stairs. Benny polished the bannister posts, which were about as tall as he was. He rubbed the dark brown wood with his cleaning cloth until it was so shiny he could see his face looking back at him.

When they were done tidying up the grand staircase, they moved on to the hallway on the second floor. Jessie swept while Benny held the dustpan. As they went, they stopped at each door. Each one had antique brass knobs, but the locks were new. None of the doors had a lock that would fit the key Juliette had given them.

One of the doors was open so that the cleaning

staff could tidy up. Jessie and Benny looked in.

"Are you the Aldens?" asked a woman who was straightening the bed. She was dressed in a hotel uniform. Jessie remembered seeing her in the lobby.

"Yes," Jessie said. "I'm Jessie and this is Benny. We were just passing by and happened to see the door was open."

"I'm Anita," the woman said. "And yes, this room will be open to the public tonight. For those who are attending the opening but not spending the night. Have you had a chance to see the rooms?"

"No, could we come in?" Jessie asked.

"Yes, of course!" said Anita.

"We won't get in your way!" said Benny.

Jessie and Benny wandered around the fancy room. It had thick, red and purple carpet. The bed had four tall posts at each corner, and it even had a canopy draped over the top of it. Old-fashioned chairs sat by the window, and against the far wall was an antique writing desk.

"Each of the rooms is unique," Anita explained. "It's not like one of the big hotels, where every room is exactly the same. That's one of the best parts about old places like this."

"Wow! So these are real antiques?" Benny asked.

Anita nodded and said, "Yes, some are over a hundred years old!"

Benny noticed an odd hissing noise that almost sounded like a whistle. He followed the noise to where a heavy-looking metal object sat under the window. The metal object had a valve on one side that was making the whistling sound. A little puff of steam came out of the valve too.

"What's that?" he asked. "It looks kind of like a metal accordion!"

"Careful, Benny, that's a radiator," Jessie said. "See the pipe in the floor? Steam comes from the boiler downstairs and in through the pipe. The steam heats the iron, which warms up the room. Be careful. They can be very hot."

Benny held his hand out to the radiator but did not to touch it. He could feel the heat coming off the metal. It felt as hot as a stove! The radiator made some more whistles and even a chirp as hot air sputtered from the valve.

"It sounds kind of like a robot!" he exclaimed.

"Old ones are especially noisy," Anita said. "Radiators like this were created in the early 1800s. People still use them in some older buildings. They're a bit old-fashioned, but they still do the job!"

Anita seemed to know a lot about the hotel. Maybe she could help them, Jessie thought. She showed Anita the old key. "We're on an errand for Juliette. We're trying to find whatever this key goes to. Have you seen anything that might match?"

Anita looked at the key and shook her head. "Juliette changed the locks when she bought the building. This key looks pretty old—definitely from before the renovation."

"That's what I was thinking," said Jessie. "If you see anything that might match the key, would you let us know? We'd really appreciate it."

"Yes, I will," Anita said.

Jessie and Benny thanked Anita and said good-bye. Back in the hallway, Benny held the dustpan and Jessie swept. The pair still had half of the hall to finish and then a whole second hall on the other side of the stairs. Thinking about so much sweeping made Benny yawn.

"I'm getting hungry, Jessie," he said. "Did you see all those snacks they're making for the party? I could really go for one...or two...or five..."

Jessie focused on sweeping, making sure she didn't miss a single inch of the hallway. She was sure it would help leave a good impression if the hallways were spotless. Not only that, they still had the whole floor to investigate.

"What do you think, Jessie? Please, can I go get a snack?" Benny asked.

Jessie paused in her sweeping to think a moment. She knew Benny might get fussy if he didn't get something to eat. Maybe it would be all right if they split up. Then again, they'd agreed to help Juliette, and teaching Benny responsibility was important.

Jessie made up her mind. She turned to Benny to let him know what she had decided.

IF JESSIE LETS BENNY GO TO THE LOBBY TO
HAVE A SNACK, GO TO PAGE 24.

IF JESSIE AND BENNY STICK TOGETHER,
GO TO PAGE 33.

BENNY'S SNACK

"All right, Benny. Once we finish sweeping the hall, you can go downstairs and find a snack," Jessie said.

"All right!" Benny cheered.

Together, Jessie and Benny swept the long hallway. By the time they reached the far end, Benny had a full dustpan and a very empty belly.

"There we go," Jessie said. "Now, take that dustpan down to the waste bin in the lobby. After that, go ahead and ask Juliette if you can have a snack. I'll finish checking the doors to see if I can find the mystery lock."

"Thanks, Jessie!" Benny said. "Don't forget to come downstairs and get a snack too."

Jessie chuckled and waved Benny off. "See you soon."

After Benny left, Jessie set her broom aside and walked up and down the halls looking at the doors. It was hard work checking everything by herself. It took her even longer than sweeping the floor, but she had promised Juliette she would investigate. By the time she had checked every door, she was pretty hungry herself. She looked out the window at the end of the hall and saw that the sun was starting to set.

Before she went downstairs to find Benny, Jessie decided to peek on the third floor, just to see what was up there. She found the stairs that went to the next floor. The steps creaked as she went up.

The third floor was very quiet. And none of the lights were on, so it was hard for Jessie to see anything in the long, empty hallway.

"Hello?" Jessie called. Her voice echoed down the hallway. "Is anyone up here?"

"Oooooh," came a soft noise from down the hallway. It sounded like a person's voice, but it was more of a sound than a word. Jessie shivered. She thought about the ghost stories Alex had told. She turned back to the stairs and went down to the first floor to find Benny.

But Benny was not in the lobby.

Juliette came up to her. "Hello, Jessie. Is something wrong?" she asked.

"No," said Jessie. She decided not to mention the sound she heard on the third floor. It was probably just the wind or maybe an old radiator. "But have you seen Benny?"

Juliette looked around. Employees were hurrying around, rearranging furniture and hanging decorations. Guests would be arriving soon.

"I told him he could go get a snack. I wonder if he met up with Henry and Violet," Jessie said.

"I just saw Henry and Violet in the kitchen having a snack," Juliette said. "You could check there. I'll let you know if I see him."

Jessie hurried to the kitchen. Inside, Henry and Violet were sitting at the preparation table, talking to the chef. The chef was tossing a salad in a big bowl.

"Jessie, there you are!" Henry said. He tilted his head. "Where's Benny?"

"That's why I came to find you," said Jessie.

"I told him he could come downstairs and get a snack, but that was a while ago. Now I can't find him anywhere."

Henry and Violet stood up.

"It's getting pretty late," said Violet. "And we haven't seen him either."

Henry was calm. "Don't worry. I'm sure he's around here. Let's ask the employees if they've seen him. But the three of us should stick together so we don't get split up even more."

Jessie, Henry, and Violet checked the hallways on the first floor. They checked Juliette's office, and when they ran into Anita, Jessie asked if she had seen Benny. She hadn't. They asked everyone, but no one had seen him. It was getting very late now, and guests were beginning to arrive for the grand opening.

"I shouldn't have let him go downstairs alone," said Jessie. "Now we've spent all evening looking for him. I'm worried!"

"Do you think he saw a ghost?" Violet asked. She thought back to the hotel's haunted rumors. She imagined Benny wandering down a dark hallway and seeing something spooky in the shadows. "If Benny saw a real ghost, he'd be sure to go chasing after it."

"It's all right, Jessie," Henry assured her. "I'm sure he's fine."

Juliette found them. She had a smile of relief on her face. "I'm glad I found you. Chef Michael wants to talk to you. I think it's about Benny," she said.

The Aldens hurried to the kitchen. The chef was waiting for them.

"I didn't think anything of it when I heard your brother was missing," he said. "But then I went to set out the cookie tray in the lobby, and I noticed a whole tray was missing."

Chef Michael showed them the counter where the cookie trays had been waiting. There was an empty spot where one of the trays had been. Violet peered at the counter and then at the floor near the counter.

"Jessie, Henry! Look at these cookie crumbs," Violet said.

Henry and Jessie looked. On the floor, a trail of crumbs and sprinkles led out the door. They all had a feeling they knew where the trail would lead. They followed it out of the kitchen.

Jessie could hear the guests arriving in the lobby. She even thought she heard Grandfather's voice.

The trail of crumbs led down the hall and into the back of the mansion near Juliette's office. The trail led right to a door they had walked by many times that evening. As Jessie opened the door, she sighed in relief.

It was a coat closet. Jackets and coats hung on hangers, but it was so full some had been piled in the corner. And asleep on the pile of fluffy coats was Benny, the empty cookie tray under his arm.

Benny woke up when they opened the door.

"Oof, good morning," he said. "I don't feel so good."

"Because you ate an entire tray of cookies!" Violet exclaimed.

"They were delicious," Benny said. "It might have been worth it."

"We've been looking everywhere for you," Jessie said. "I'm so glad you're all right."

They were interrupted by a commotion coming

from the lobby. Henry helped Benny up, and the four Alden children hurried to see what was going on. By the time they got there, people were rushing out the door. Everyone was pale with fright.

"The stories are true!" cried one of the guests. "The ghost of the Lost Composer!"

Four of the people leaving were a group of well-dressed men and women wearing blazers with the historical committee emblem. They weren't frightened, but they were not happy. As the guests left and the room got quieter, another noise could be heard.

It was music—creepy organ music—as though the organ pipes were playing all by themselves!

"Please, let me explain!" Juliette called after the guests, but they continued to leave.

"This kind of commotion is very unprofessional," said one of the men from the historical committee.

"What happened?" Henry asked.

"I don't know," Juliette said. "The pipe organ just started playing all by itself. I don't know how this could happen without the keyboard!"

"Wait a minute," Jessie said. She made her way

through the crowd, and Henry, Violet, and Benny followed. They stopped next to an old record player near the wall of the lobby. The needle was spinning around a record that said, "The Greatest Works of Charles Ivy."

"The music isn't coming from the organ at all," Jessie said. "Even though it sounds like organ music." She lifted up the record needle, and the music stopped.

"Well, even if it's not a ghost, it looks like it worked," Henry said.

Henry sighed. The children watched helplessly as the last guest ran out of the lobby.

THE END

TO FOLLOW A DIFFERENT PATH, GO TO PAGE 23.

STICKING TOGETHER

"Let's stay together, Benny," Jessie said. "The work will be easier and get done faster that way. Then when we're done, we can go down to the kitchen for snacks."

Benny was disappointed but only for a moment. If they could get the work done faster, then they could have snacks faster too.

"Okay!" he said.

They finished sweeping the hall and set the broom and dustpan aside. Then they walked up and down the halls looking at the locks on the doors. Each of the rooms had new locks. None of them matched the mystery key. Just when Benny was about to ask if they could go down to the kitchen, he heard a noise. It sounded like jingling!

Benny grabbed Jessie's hand. He remembered Alex's ghost story and imagined the ghost of the boy wandering the halls and jangling his keys.

"Jessie, do you hear that?" he asked.

Jessie listened closely.

"Yes, I do," she said after a moment. "It sounds like keys, or maybe a little bell. I think it's coming from the third floor. Let's check it out."

Jessie and Benny followed the noise upstairs. The third floor was dark and quiet.

"Hello?" Jessie called into the shadows. "Anyone up here?"

"Shh!" said Benny. "I hear the jangling again!"

Both of them covered their mouths and listened. They could hear the metallic sound of jingling. And not only that, but the clunking sounds of heavy footsteps.

"The Lost Composer!" Benny whispered.

"I'm not so sure," Jessie said. She could hear something else besides the jingling and footsteps. It sounded like whispering. "Come on. Let's check it out together."

Benny followed Jessie, holding on to her sleeve

as she walked down the hall. In the dark, all the old furniture and paintings were much spookier than the ones downstairs. The children's footsteps tap-tap-tapped on the wood floor. The jingling and stomping got louder.

At the end of the hallway was a big mirror. It was very old and so dusty that Benny could hardly see his reflection in it. He stepped up to the mirror and wiped some of the dust away with his hand. Then he jumped when the mirror's glass flickered, as if a shadow had passed through it! Before he could tell Jessie, she called to him.

"Benny, over here," she said. She was pointing to one of the doors closest to the end of the hall. It was cracked open, and Benny could see the lights flickering inside. The jingling became louder, and Benny could hear a deep voice coming from inside the room.

"Oooooh! Oooooh!" said the voice in a low moan. It sounded just like a ghost!

Benny shook Jessie's hand. "It's the ghost," he said. "He's in that room! What will happen if he finds us? Will he take the key?"

Jessie wasn't afraid. In fact, she walked right up to the door and opened it.

"It's not a ghost at all, Benny," said Jessie.

Benny peeked around the door.

Inside were two teenagers with a video camera. One was filming while the other was standing near the light switch, flipping it on and off. They had a ring of keys hanging from the ceiling on a string so it looked like they were floating.

"See, Benny? It's just people making a video," said Jessie.

The teenagers were startled to see Jessie and Benny.

"Oh!" said the girl with the camera. "You scared me! I didn't see you there."

"You scared me too!" Benny said. "I thought you were a ghost."

"I *wish*," said the boy standing by the light switch. He was wearing heavy shoes, and when he stepped away from the switch, his steps were loud and clunking. Just like Benny had heard from the hallway. "Then we could film a real ghost instead of having to fake it."

"Sorry we scared you," added the girl. "I'm Kylie, and this is my brother, Luke."

"You're making a movie about ghosts?" Jessie asked.

Luke nodded. "Yeah. Our aunt Anita works here and told us all about the stories of the Lost Composer. We wanted to get footage of a real ghost...but we haven't had any luck."

"So we decided to make a video anyway," Kylie said. "Have you heard about the Lost Composer?"

"Yeah, I know all about the Lost Composer!" Benny said. "But the keys are supposed to be *invisible*. The ghost story says whenever people hear the keys, they look in the hallway but no one's there!"

Luke sighed again, and Kylie made a smug face.

"I told you they were supposed to be invisible," she said.

"I think we'll get more likes on our video if the keys are floating," said Luke. "It's more dramatic."

"Not if you can see the string. I told you we should have used fishing line!" said Kylie.

"Say," Jessie said, trying to get their attention. "You two didn't write a message to Juliette about some keys, did you?"

"What?" Kylie asked. "No, what do you mean?"

"Someone wrote a message trying to frighten Juliette into giving over some keys."

Luke frowned. "No way. We'd never try to scare Juliette."

"I think they're telling the truth," Benny whispered to Jessie. "Plus, Juliette would never be tricked by keys hanging from the ceiling on string."

Benny was right. It didn't seem like Luke and Kylie had written the message, so Jessie waved good-bye. "Well, we'll let you get back to your ghost movie," she said. "Good luck getting a lot of likes."

As they left the room, Benny looked at the big mirror at the end of the hallway again. This time, instead of a shadow, he saw a *cat*!

"Jessie, the mirror!" he said.

Jessie gasped. She saw it too! Kylie and Luke hurried over. All four of them could see the shape of a cat in the reflection of the mirror, but there was no cat in the hallway. The cat in the mirror had long, black fur and bright yellow eyes. And it was staring right at them!

"I've got to get this on film!" Kylie said. But before she could start recording on her camera, the cat jumped away and disappeared.

"Did you guys do that?" Jessie asked. "Is that part of your ghost video?"

"No way! We don't have the technology for that!" said Luke. His eyes were big like he'd seen a ghost. Maybe they had. "I think we just saw a real one!"

"This is Room 322, after all," Kylie whispered. "It's right above Room 222, where Aunt Anita says guests used to report loud knocking and jangling noises in the night. We were hoping if we stayed here we'd hear them, but now I don't know if I want to!"

Jessie and Benny glanced at each other when Kylie mentioned Room 222. That was the room they were supposed to take the keys to, according to the message Juliette had received.

"Let's all start by going downstairs and away from this creepy mirror," Jessie said.

Benny nodded. Jessie always had good ideas, and that was the best one he'd heard that day. The four of them left the dark hallway and went downstairs. When they reached the grand staircase on the second floor, they could see down into the lobby. Guests were slowly arriving.

"I've changed my mind," said Luke. "If this hotel really is haunted, I don't think I want to stay here."

"Me either," said Kylie. "It was nice meeting you two, but I think we're going to go home. See you."

Kylie and Luke waved and hurried down the stairs. Jessie shook her head. She and her siblings had seen some pretty amazing things in the past, but she still couldn't explain the sight of the cat in the mirror. She reminded herself there had to be a reasonable explanation.

Benny saw Henry and Violet putting away their cleaning supplies and heading toward the kitchen.

"Jessie, look. Henry and Violet are going to the kitchen," Benny said.

"We both know what that means," Jessie said. She was excited to share what they'd seen with Henry and Violet. "Snack time!"

CONTINUE TO PAGE 53

THE BASEMENT

Henry carried the vacuum to the lobby, and Violet brought window cleaner and paper towels. While Henry vacuumed the entryway carpets, Violet cleaned the windows that faced the driveway until they were sparkling and clear. Then they both helped Alex prop open the front doors so the hotel would be inviting when the guests arrived.

"Do you really think the hotel is haunted?" Violet asked Alex as they stood back and looked at the entrance to the hotel. With the doors open and all the decorations, it looked fabulous. Henry finished tying some balloons to the handrails leading up to the doors.

"I don't know," said Alex. "I grew up in town, so we always told ghost stories about the mansion when we were kids. It's very well known in the area, and a lot of teens would sneak in searching for ghosts back when it was old Charles Gardner running the hotel."

"Did you ever hear the jingling of the Lost Composer's keys?" Henry asked.

Alex laughed. "No," he said. "But I did get lost in the hedge maze once."

"The hedge maze!" Violet said. "What's that?"

Henry and Violet followed him around to the side of the mansion. The back of the hotel reminded Henry of Grandfather's garden, where their boxcar was. The Gardner Hotel had a big garden filled with well-trimmed hedges that formed a maze. The green walls of the maze were tall enough that when Henry stood next to one, the hedge came up to his shoulders.

"Wow!" said Henry. "I've never seen a real hedge maze."

"It's just like something out of *Alice in Wonderland*," Violet said. She was shorter than Henry, so the hedge was almost as tall as she was. She reached out and touched the waxy green leaves. The walls were made out of holly and were quite prickly.

"Maybe we can explore it tomorrow morning," Henry said. "Grandfather said we could spend the night. But for now, we should probably get back inside and keep looking for the lock that matches this key. I'd like to get to the bottom of this mystery well before midnight."

They headed back toward the front entrance of the hotel. As they came around the side of the hotel, Violet noticed a strange wooden door that looked like it might open right into the ground. "What's that?" she asked

"I think that's a cellar door," Henry said. "Grandfather's house has one too, out in the garden."

"Yes, the door leads to an old cellar in the basement. But no one uses the cellar anymore," Alex said. Then he checked his watch. "Uh-oh, I should get back to work."

"Is there another way to get into the basement?" Henry asked. "I thought we could search there to see if this key goes to anything."

"Yes, there's another door that goes to the

basement inside the hotel," said Alex. "But we keep that door locked too. I'll try to find Juliette and ask if she'll give me the keys so I can let you in. I'll come find you then."

Henry was about to follow Alex inside when Violet tapped him on the arm. She walked over to the old cellar door.

"Look," she said. Violet pointed at the door's latch. It was hanging open. "The latch is open, but didn't Alex just say no one uses the cellar anymore?"

"Hmm, you're right," Henry said. "Let's take a look."

Henry stooped and pulled open the heavy door. Behind it was a set of stairs leading down into cellar.

"Are you sure it's safe?" Violet asked.

"Yes. Just be careful on the stairs," Henry said.

The two of them felt their way down into the dark and damp cellar. The room was empty, like Alex had said—no secret locks for the mysterious old keys. Using the light streaming in from the open door, Henry and Violet made their way across the room to another door, which opened into the basement hallway.

Henry found a light switch and turned it on. Even with the light, it was dim. The hallway smelled musty and reminded Henry of Grandfather's basement. The walls were gray brick, and the floor was concrete. There were cobwebs in every corner.

On one end of the hallway, stairs led up into the hotel. At the other end was a big metal door.

Violet saw a spider scurry across the floor and took a step closer to Henry.

"Don't worry," said Henry. "Even in old mansions, all basements seem the same, don't they? Dark and a bit creepy. Other than that, it's just like any old basement. If we can find what the mystery keys unlock, we'll be one step closer to finding out who wrote that message and what they want."

"It does seem like the kind of place we might find something with an old lock," she said, nodding.

"Wow, look at these footprints," Henry said. The prints were muddy gray and led right up to the big metal door. Henry crouched down and noticed hot air blowing across the floor. It was coming from the metal door, which was open slightly. "I think these prints are fresh," he said.

Violet crouched next to him. "How do you know?"

"If the prints were old, the mud would have dried a long time ago from this hot air," he said. "But the mud is still wet."

Henry pushed the door open. "Hello?" he called. "Anybody down here?"

There was a big metal boiler at the far end of the room. On the wall were electrical panels and a fuse box.

"The hot air must be coming from the boiler," Violet said, looking at the big metal contraption. "It doesn't seem like it should be blowing all that air and making those sounds."

"Let's check it out," Henry said. "If the boiler's broken, that would be pretty bad. And I bet Juliette is probably too busy with the grand opening to notice."

The air got hotter as they got closer. A wrench was hanging from a bolt on the boiler, as if someone had been trying to adjust it, and the doors to the fuse boxes were open.

"Maybe that's why the cellar door was open. Was

someone trying to fix the boiler?" Henry wondered out loud. It was quite warm.

Violet didn't see anything that had a lock on it.

"Let's go back upstairs and find Jessie and Benny," said Violet. "There's something weird going on down here, and I don't like it."

"There are just a few nuts loose," said Henry. "I think I might be able to tighten them myself." Then he hesitated. He had helped Grandfather fix some things in their boiler room at home, but he wasn't sure if he knew what he was doing.

Henry turned to Violet. "Maybe you're right and we should go back and tell Juliette. What do you think?"

IF HENRY TRIES TO FIX THE BOILER, GO TO PAGE 50.

IF HENRY AND VIOLET SHUT THE BOILER ROOM DOOR AND GO BACK UPSTAIRS, GO TO PAGE 53.

FIXING THE BOILER

"You really think you can fix it?" Violet asked.

"I'll give it a try," Henry decided. He picked up the wrench. Suddenly, the lights went out. It was pitch dark! Violet grabbed Henry's hand. Through the inky shadows she heard something. It sounded like the jingling of keys!

"Could it be the Lost Composer?" she whispered.

"That's just a ghost story," Henry said. He held Violet's hand and felt along the wall with his other hand. He was calm. He called into the shadows, "Who's up there? Hello?"

"Bring the keys to Room 222 by midnight," came a deep, low whisper. "Or I'll scare all the guests out of the hotel!"

"Who are you?" Henry called. "Why do you want

to ruin the grand opening?"

The voice didn't answer. Henry and Violet both heard the jangling of keys again, and then wood creaking from the cellar door. A moment later there was a loud *SLAM*.

"Oh no, Henry!" Violet said. "The cellar door!"

They found the door, but it was too late. They heard someone close the latch from the outside. The door into the garden was locked shut. Henry grunted and felt along the wall for the light switch. After a moment, he found it. They both let out sighs of relief. Violet felt her heart pounding.

"That was scary!" she said.

"I know," said Henry. "I'm glad we're all right, even if the door out is shut. Come on. Let's try the door at the top of the stairs. The one that goes into the hotel."

Violet followed Henry up the old, creaky stairs. Henry tried the door, but it was locked, just like Alex had said. Through the door, they could hear distant voices of people inside the hotel, but no one was close enough to hear them when Henry pounded on the thick door.

"Whoever was down here sure didn't want us to find out who they were," Henry said. "We were so close! Now we'll have to wait for Alex to find those keys and hope he tries looking for us down here. But with the party going on, it could be a while."

Henry and Violet sat down on the stairs to wait until they heard someone come by. They would never solve the mystery now!

THE END

TO FOLLOW A DIFFERENT PATH, GO TO PAGE 49.

THE ALDENS REGROUP

Henry and Violet saw Jessie and Benny come down the grand staircase into the lobby. The grandfather clock rang six o'clock just as Alex, Anita, and Juliette were putting the finishing touches on the decorations. Guests would be arriving in one hour! The children met at the foot of the stairs.

"Let's go to the kitchen to talk," said Jessie. "Benny got hungry while we were upstairs, and I think we could all use a snack."

The four of them went into the kitchen. The chef looked very busy, so the children patiently waited for him to finish what he was doing. As the Aldens watched, the man opened a door on the wall and loaded two trays of food into a metal box. Then he closed the door and pressed a button.

Benny watched in wonder. "Is that a food elevator?" he asked. He imagined what it would be like to have an elevator deliver Mrs. McGregor's pancakes to his room every morning.

Henry smiled. "It kind of is," he said. "It's called a dumbwaiter. They used to be common in mansions like this. The chef must be sending food to another floor in the building."

"That's right," said Jessie. "They will be showing off some of the rooms on the second floor later. They probably need food up there, and with a dumbwaiter, no one needs to carry the trays up stairs."

A moment later the chef came over to the children with another tray. There were fancy ham-and-cheese sandwiches, olives with garlic inside, and a half dozen other things on the tray.

"You're the Aldens, aren't you?" the chef asked. "Juliette told me you would want snacks. This is a taste test of the treats I've made for the guests this evening. Please let me know how everything is!"

Benny had already eaten two olives. "So far so

good!" he said. They all laughed.

After the chef went back to preparing the food for the party, Benny swallowed the bite in his mouth and said, "Have we got news to tell you!"

"Same!" Violet said. "You go first."

"When Jessie and I were upstairs, we heard some noises," said Benny. "We went up to the third floor and thought we heard a ghost! I thought it was the Lost Composer for sure!"

"But it turned out to be some older kids pretending to be ghosts so they could get likes on their video channel," Jessie said. "Then the strangest thing happened. We saw what looked like the reflection of a cat inside a mirror. But there was no cat in the hallway!"

"Did it look like a ghost?" Violet asked.

"I'm not sure," Jessie said. "I can't explain it though. What about you two?"

"We went down to the basement," Henry said.

"We saw some muddy boot prints leading to the boiler room," said Violet. "We shut the door and came back upstairs. It was dark and creepy down there!"

"The boiler room door was left open, and I saw a wrench out. At first, I thought there was a problem someone was trying to fix, but the more I think about it, the more I think someone might actually be trying to break it."

"Breaking the boiler could cause all sorts of problems for Juliette's party," Jessie said. "You know, I was thinking about all of this after we met Luke and Kylie pretending to be ghosts. Think about the message Juliette got: 'bring my keys to Room 222 or I will not rest.' I think it's a person pretending to be the Lost Composer and trying to scare Juliette into giving up those keys."

"Or at least scare her guests who believe the ghost stories," Henry said. "No guests means no business, and it will probably mean the historical committee won't put the building on the historical registry."

"What's a historical committee, anyway?" Benny asked.

"The historical committee is in charge of a list of historic places," Jessie explained. "That means if they decide the building should be a historical landmark it will be put on a list that is recognized by the government."

"It would be pretty sad for Juliette if the committee decided not to register the building because of the broken boiler," Henry said.

"Then do you think whoever is behind the message could be trying to break the boiler?" Violet asked. "As a way to convince Juliette to hand over the keys?"

"We saw the radiators upstairs," Benny said. "They made some pretty weird noises. And some steam puffed out too! If I didn't know what it was, I might think it was a ghost."

As they left the kitchen and returned to the lobby, Violet noticed a man walk in through the front doors. It did not look like he was dressed for a fancy party. He wore jeans and a sweatshirt under a worn-out jacket.

"His boots," Violet whispered.

The man was wearing heavy-duty boots, and the bottoms were caked with mud.

"The muddy footprints downstairs?" Benny asked.

Juliette saw the man come in and walked out to meet him. Even though she was friendly as they spoke, the man didn't smile. They talked for a minute. Then the man walked past Juliette and left. Juliette looked at the floor where the man had been standing. His boots had left mud on the tile.

Juliette came over to the Aldens.

"I'm sorry to ask after you did such a good job cleaning, but could I ask you for one more favor?" she said. "Would you sweep up the lobby one more time? I'd do it myself, but we're getting so close to the party."

"No problem," Henry said. "Who was that man?"

"His name is Sebastian," said Juliette. "He was the hotel's maintenance person before it closed. I feel bad...he was laid off so suddenly. I couldn't afford to rehire him, but I invited him to the opening because I know he loves the hotel."

"Does he always wear muddy boots?" Benny asked.

Juliette chuckled. "I've never seen him without them. I think having muddy boots is something people get used to when they work on old buildings."

"We'll clean up the lobby right away," Henry said. "By the way, I meant to tell you—Violet and I went into the basement. We didn't find any secret locks, but we did notice the boiler room was open, and there was a lot of hot air coming out."

"Oh no," said Juliette. "That old thing is on its last legs. It's been acting up lately. Thanks for telling me. I'll ask Anita to check it out."

Juliette hurried away. She was in a rush now that it was getting close to the start of the party. Jessie got the broom from the closet, and the four of them studied the boot prints in the lobby before they swept them up.

"What do you think? Do they match the prints you found downstairs?" Jessie asked.

Violet looked closely and nodded. The prints were a match.

"I'd ask what a maintenance man was doing in the boiler room, but maybe he was just trying to fix the old thing," Henry said.

Jessie swept up the prints, and Benny rubbed the tiles with a cloth until they shined.

"But Juliette said she wasn't able to rehire him,"

Jessie said. "Why would he try to fix something if he wasn't hired to?"

"She did say he loves the hotel. Maybe he wanted to fix it because he cares about the building," Violet suggested.

They went to the closet to put the broom away. Henry tapped his chin with a finger, thinking.

"It still doesn't make sense to me," he said. "There was a lot of hot air coming out of the boiler room. If Sebastian were trying to fix the boiler, why would he have left it when it was still blowing all that hot air?"

"And we still don't know about the cat we saw in the mirror!" Benny said.

Violet shivered. "And we're not any closer to figuring out who wrote that message," she said.

"I think we are closer, in fact," said Jessie. "Let's go over what we know so far."

"Someone wants to ruin Juliette's grand opening in order to get these mystery keys," Henry said.

"But we don't know who or why!" Benny added.

"They want keys brought to Room 222," Violet said. "Which is also a room that is not in service."

"It's also supposed to be the most haunted room," Jessie said.

Henry nodded. "So, whoever wrote the message knows a lot about the hotel's history and the ghost stories. Do we know any suspects who fit that description?"

"Eddie Gardner seemed grumpy about the way Juliette is running the hotel," Violet suggested. "Also, he had that bag that looked like it wiggled, which was strange."

"And we can't forget Sebastian," Jessie said. "His boot prints matched what you two saw downstairs. I don't know why he might want to ruin the grand opening, but he did lose his job when the hotel first closed. Maybe he is upset Juliette didn't rehire him."

"And both of them know things about this building," Henry said. "Eddie lived in the hotel as a child, and if Sebastian did maintenance on it, he would have spent a lot of time here too."

"I just can't stop thinking about that cat we saw in the mirror," Jessie said. "Everything else has an explanation, but that was just spooky. And it was right above Room 222."

A group of two men and two women came in through the front door. They were dressed in jackets with the historical committee emblem embroidered on the lapel. One of the men had a bushy white mustache that reminded Violet of something out of a history book. One of the women was wearing an eyeglass in one eye.

"The historical committee!" Violet said in a hushed voice.

Juliette met the group and introduced herself. She shook their hands and started showing them around the lobby. The woman with the single eyeglass was taking notes on a pad. All four members of the committee were very serious, looking at every detail of the old building.

"I'm glad we got those muddy prints cleaned up," Benny said. "They would have noticed right away!"

Henry glanced at the clock. They still had quite a bit of time before midnight.

"Let's get out of the way so Juliette can show the committee around," he said.

"What do you think we should do?" Jessie asked.

Henry smiled, his eyes sparkling with a daring idea.

"I think there's one area of the hotel we haven't explored. And it's pretty important to this mystery," he said. "Let's go to Room 222."

CONTINUE TO PAGE 64

ROOM 222

The children slipped upstairs while Juliette was showing the historical committee around the lobby. Juliette was very serious but friendly while she talked to the committee.

"The committee's approval means a lot to her," Henry said as the children walked.

"It seems strange that either Eddie or Sebastian would want to stop the building from becoming a landmark," Violet said. "I feel like Eddie would want that for his father, and if Sebastian really does love the hotel, he would want that to happen too."

"I think we're missing something," said Jessie. "Hopefully we can find some answers in Room 222."

"And maybe a ghost cat!" said Benny.

The Aldens reached the second-floor landing. When Jessie and Benny explored the second floor before, they'd met Anita. This time the hallway felt different. It was empty and quiet. All the doors were closed. Violet thought there was something spooky about the way everything looked the same.

Benny led the way. Suddenly, he noticed something move at the end of the hallway. But when he looked he saw that it was just the children's reflections. On the far wall was another big, oval mirror.

"That mirror looks just like the one I saw upstairs—the one with the ghost cat," Benny said. "But it's cleaner, and it doesn't look quite so creepy."

They found a door at the end of the hallway, near the mirror. Jessie read the number.

"Yep," she said. "Just like Luke and Kylie said. This is Room 222, right below Room 322, where we saw the cat in the mirror."

Benny and Violet looked into the mirror, but all they saw were their reflections.

"I don't see any ghost cats," Benny said. He was a little disappointed.

"Do you think you imagined it?" Violet asked. She did not take her eyes away from the mirror.

"No, both of us saw it," Jessie said. "It was definitely a cat with long black fur."

Henry leaned in close to the mirror. He held his hands up and peered through it like a window.

"I don't know," he said. "I can't see any—"

KNOCK, KNOCK, KNOCK!

Benny yelped as a loud noise rang out. It sounded like it was close by, but everything in the hallway was still.

Then Violet noticed something in the mirror. "Look!" she said, and as she pointed, a shadow seemed to pass through the glass. Again, there was no sign of movement in the hallway.

"That was no ghost cat!" Benny cried. "It's the Lost Composer!"

Jessie shushed him and motioned toward the door of Room 222. For the first time, she noticed the door was slightly ajar. A draft of cool air puffed out, and the door creaked open slowly. Benny grabbed Henry's hand, but no one came out of the door. Not even a ghost.

"I don't think it's a ghost, Benny," said Henry. "The door must not have been latched all the way. The wind blew it open. Should we check it out?"

Jessie opened the door all the way. And Benny could see that it looked like a regular room—maybe even a little more interesting.

"Okay," he said. "But you go first."

Room 222 was bigger than the other hotel rooms they'd seen. It had a sitting area with two old chairs, a fireplace, and a bookshelf. One of the windows was cracked open, and the evening wind gently blew the curtains.

Henry checked the bathroom and closet for any clues. Meanwhile, Jessie searched around the bedroom—even looking under the beds. Nothing seemed out of place.

Violet was the first to notice something strange. She was looking at the rocking chair by the fireplace. At first, she thought the breeze from the window was making it move, but as it slowly stopped rocking, she realized something else had been moving it.

"I think someone was just sitting in that chair!" she said.

Benny noticed something else. "Do ghosts need to stay warm?" he asked. He was kneeling by fireplace, where there was still the faint glow of flames and a crackling of burning wood.

"Good observations, you two," said Jessie. "There must have been someone here. They must have left when they heard us in the hallway."

"But we were right outside the door!" said Benny. "Where did they go? And why did the door blow open?"

Henry walked over to the door that went to the hallway. He pulled it shut until the latch clicked. Then he pressed gently against the door. The door's latch slipped, and the door opened right up.

"The latch is loose," Henry said. "Whoever was here forgot to lock it. All it would take is a little puff of air for the door to open out to the hallway."

"Do you think they left through the window?" Violet asked.

"I don't think so," said Henry. "It's pretty high

up. But remember that wind that blew the hallway door open? It could have been caused by another door opening and closing. My guess is there's a hidden way out of this room. Let's see if we can find it."

The four children split up to explore the room more closely. Before long, Benny found another clue. Three books had fallen off the shelf into a pile. He stooped to pick them up. Then he and Henry tried to figure out where they fit back on the shelf.

"Here's a space for four books," Henry said. "Three fell, but the last book is sitting right in the middle of the space."

On the shelf there was a gap with a single book standing upright.

"If someone knocked the other books down, don't you think they would have knocked that one down too?" Benny asked. Henry nodded as Jessie and Violet joined them. He reached out and grabbed the lonely book.

"It's stuck!" he said. He tried pulling at it by the spine. It slid out slowly, like it was stuck. When he let go, it flew back toward the shelf with a loud KNOCK!

"The knocking noise!" Violet gasped.

"Knock, knock, knock!" Benny said. "Three times!"

Henry grinned. They were onto something! He pulled on the book two more times and let it snap back into place. KNOCK, KNOCK!

On the third knock, the bookcase rumbled. Then it popped open. Behind it was a secret doorway!

"Now we know what the knocking sound is," Jessie said. "Someone was opening this secret doorway!"

Henry peered inside. There was a narrow hallway beyond the bookcase. It was dark but clean, and it was lit by a few lights hanging from the ceiling.

"A secret hallway," Benny exclaimed.

"Let's see where it goes," Henry said. "Maybe we can catch up with whoever left."

The four followed the corridor. After a little ways, the children found a large oval mirror set

into the wall. Jessie examined it.

"It's just like the mirror in the main hallway," she said. "Oh, look at this!"

The other three quickly joined her and looked into the mirror. But instead of it showing their reflections, it was clear as a window. They could see out into the hallway, where they had been standing only a few minutes ago!

"It's a two-way mirror!" Jessie said. "We can see through it in this direction, but from the hallway it looks like a mirror."

"I bet if the light hits it just right, you can still see through it from the hallway side," Henry said, glancing up at the hanging lights.

"So the shadow we saw was the person that was leaving," said Violet.

"That means the cat we saw on the third floor was probably real," said Benny. He sounded a little disappointed. "It was just on the other side of a two-way mirror."

"But I thought cats weren't allowed in the hotel," Violet said.

Henry glanced back at Violet with a knowing nod.

"Let's see where this hallway goes," he said.

The hallway ended with a set of wood stairs. The children climbed the stairs and opened the door at the top. When they stepped out, they were in a large room with a big desk and bookshelves full of old books. Just like Benny thought, there was another two-way mirror on the wall. He looked out and could see into the hallway where he, Jessie, Luke, and Kylie had seen the cat.

"The cat must have been sitting right here on this bookshelf!" he said.

Meanwhile, Violet read the covers in one stack of books piled on the chair near where they were standing.

"Music," she said. "Books of sheet music?"

"It looks like a music room," Jessie said. "I think I even see an old keyboard over there!"

"This is a book of compositions by Charles Ivy," Violet said.

Jessie sorted through the papers on the desk. They had music staffs drawn on them, marked up with music and handwritten notes.

"This says the composer is Charles Ivy too,"

Jessie said. "Could this somehow be Charles Ivy's music room?"

Violet thought of something. "Remember the ghost story Alex told about the Lost Composer?" she asked. "He said whenever the organ played by itself, it would only play music by Charles Ivy."

"Charles Ivy *was* mainly an organist," Henry said.

"The organ downstairs!" Benny exclaimed.

Suddenly, Jessie held a finger up to her mouth.

"Shh!" she said. "Do you hear something?"

They all kept quiet and listened. Sure enough, there was a faint humming noise coming from the far wall of the secret room.

Henry noticed there was a silver door on the wall. It looked like the one they had seen in the kitchen but older.

"It's the dumbwaiter," said Henry. "It goes all the way up to the third floor!"

"Do you think whoever we followed up here is using it to escape?" asked Violet.

"Or maybe the ghost just got hungry and ordered some food!" said Benny.

"If there is a person inside, we might be able to make it downstairs in time to see who was up here," said Jessie.

IF THE ALDENS CONTINUE TO SEARCH FOR CLUES IN THE SECRET ROOM, GO TO PAGE 76.

IF THE ALDENS LEAVE TO CHASE THE DUMBWAITER, GO TO PAGE 82.

SEARCHING THE SECRET ROOM

The humming of the dumbwaiter stopped.

"Let's finish looking through this room," said Henry. "Then we can go back downstairs."

Violet carefully paged through some of the sheet music books. The covers were worn, and the pages had a soft, musty smell like the old books in the library.

"Isn't Eddie's father named Charles?" Benny asked. He remembered when Juliette had told them about the hotel's history. "Charles Gardner— the person that owned the hotel before Juliette?"

Jessie found something else. She held up a picture frame with a newspaper clipping. The man in the news photo had the same thick eyebrows as Eddie. He was seated in front of a big pipe organ. The headline on the paper read, "Composer Charles Ivy to Play at Symphony Hall."

"I think they're the same," Jessie said. "I think Eddie's father was Charles Ivy, the famous composer."

"To think, he owned this hotel too!" Violet said. "This must be where he went to compose all his music."

"Check this out!" Benny said. He was standing near a keyboard set up by the window. "It doesn't look like any piano I've ever seen."

Henry glanced out the window. It was getting dark out. From the third floor, he had a good view of the driveway in front of the hotel, and he could see it filling with cars as guests arrived. Jessie and Violet joined him, and they watched Juliette greet guests on the front steps. Everyone was dressed in suits and gowns.

"There's Grandfather!" Jessie said.

Grandfather was wearing a suit with a bow tie. He found Juliette to say hello and then headed inside.

"He's so handsome when he dresses up," Violet said.

"Too bad he almost never does!" Henry joked, and they laughed.

The crowd of people moved slowly inside, where the grand opening party was about to start. Soon they would all be in the lobby enjoying snacks and the beautiful hotel Juliette had worked so hard to prepare.

"We should keep looking," Henry said. "It's getting late. If we don't find out who's trying to get hold of these mystery keys, it's going to be midnight before we know it. I'm sure if we keep trying we'll be able to solve this puzzle."

"Right," said Jessie. "We should check out that jingling noise we heard."

"Speaking of noises, do you hear that?" Violet asked, tilting her head.

The three of them listened. It sounded like organ music coming from downstairs.

"You guys, this piano is broken," said Benny. "I'm trying to play the song I know, but no sounds are coming out!"

He was sitting on the old bench, and as he pressed the keys, no noise came out of the keyboard.

Instead, the sound was coming out of the organ downstairs in the lobby!

Jessie's cheeks flushed. "Oh no! Benny, stop playing!" she said.

Benny stopped playing right away, but it was too late. The four Aldens gathered at the window and looked down into the driveway. The hotel guests were rushing out of the lobby. Some of them were shouting in fear. Henry opened the window so they could hear more clearly.

"The organ!" one of the guests cried. "The organ was playing by itself!"

"The hotel is haunted after all!" yelled another. "The Lost Composer!"

Juliette came running out onto the front steps. "I'm sure there's an explanation!" she called after them. "Please, come back!"

Grandfather tried to help Juliette convince the guests to stay, but everyone was too frightened.

"But the organ isn't haunted at all," Jessie said. "It was just Benny playing on a keyboard!"

"I didn't know!" said Benny.

"None of us did, Benny," said Jessie. "It must

be connected to the organ in the lobby somehow...
We've got to go down and tell them!"

Henry shook his head. "I think it might be too
late," he said.

They watched the guests get into their cars and
drive away. The last people to leave were the four
members of the historical committee.

THE END

TO FOLLOW A DIFFERENT PATH, GO TO PAGE 75.

CHASING THE DUMBWAITER

"Let's see if we can get downstairs to figure out if someone was just here," said Jessie.

The children hurried out of the secret room, down the secret stairway, and back into Room 222. Jessie, Henry, and Violet were already in the main hallway when they noticed Benny was no longer with them.

"Benny, come on!" Jessie called. "We need to figure out who was just here."

She went back into Room 222 and found Benny standing next to the open window.

"Do you hear that?" Benny asked. "It sounds like jingling!"

Jessie, Henry, and Violet joined Benny at the window and looked out. In addition to the jingling, they saw a shadow moving quickly through the garden and into the hedge maze.

"Good ears, Benny," said Henry. "We probably won't be able to make it downstairs in time to check the dumbwaiter, but I think we just found another lead. If we follow the sound, we might find out who's trying to scare Juliette's guests!"

Back through the hall the children went, and down the grand staircase. They were careful not to bump into anyone as they crossed through the lobby and went out the front door. Juliette was outside greeting guests as they arrived, and the driveway was filling with cars as more people arrived. Everyone was dressed in suits and gowns.

"There's Grandfather!" Jessie said.

Grandfather was wearing a suit with a bow tie. "Why are you four in such a hurry?" he asked.

"We've got an important lead on our case," Violet explained. "We'll be back soon!"

"Seems you four are always on the case," Grandfather said with a chuckle. "Stay together and be safe!"

They waved to Grandfather and hurried on their

way. Henry and Violet led Jessie and Benny around the side of the building.

"Alex showed us the hedge maze earlier," Henry explained. "I'm sure whatever we saw escaping was headed in that direction!"

The small green leaves of the hedges glistened in the lights from the back patio. The sun had gone down. It was getting late.

Benny pointed. "I hear jingling that way!" he said.

"All right, but let's stick together so we don't get lost," Jessie said.

Together, they went into the hedge maze. Henry was just tall enough to see over the top of the hedges, but he couldn't see anyone else in the maze. The bushes were dense and prickly, and the darker it got the more difficult it was to see the path. They followed Benny, who followed the sound of the jingling.

Suddenly the sound stopped.

"I think whatever it was got away," Benny said. "If it's not a ghost, I want to know what it really was."

"What's that?" Violet asked. Ahead, the hedges

opened into a clearing at the middle of the maze. They walked into the clearing and found an old shed. A shovel and a rake leaned against the shed next to a coiled-up garden hose.

"Must be the gardener's shed," said Henry.

"It's pretty old," Violet said. "Do you think whatever these keys go to could be inside?"

"Since we're here, we might as well check inside," Jessie said. She looked over her shoulder. The hotel's silhouette was black against the dark blue sky. Warm, gold light shone out from the windows and the lobby.

"But let's not take too long," Jessie said. "It's getting late."

Henry opened the door to the shed. It wasn't locked. Inside were more gardening tools. A hedge clipper hung on the wall, and some bags of fertilizer and soil were stacked in the corner. There was also a workshop table and an old metal toolbox full of wrenches and screwdrivers. Although the shed looked old, the supplies were fairly new, like the tools Mrs. McGregor had stored in the gardening shed at Grandfather's house.

"Hey, what's this?" Benny asked.

Under a pile of plastic tarps, Benny found a heavy metal chest. Unlike the tools in the shed, the chest was very old. It had rusted bands on the top and was very dusty. There were some fresh marks on the metal bands, like someone had tried to break it open.

"The lock!" Violet exclaimed.

A big padlock dangled from the chest's latch. It was iron and had an old-fashioned keyhole—a keyhole that was very familiar! Henry took the key from his pocket and handed it to Violet.

"Give it a try," he said.

Violet put the key in the lock and turned. It was a little sticky, but with some effort she was able to twist it. The lock clunked open.

"It's like a treasure chest!" said Benny. "I wonder what's inside!"

Together, Violet and Benny opened the chest. Even though the chest looked old, inside they found a collection of cell phones, keys, and jewelry. There were also a few credit cards and even a leather wallet full of cash.

"What is all this?" Benny asked. "I guess it's kind of like treasure. That's a lot of money in that wallet."

All the items in the chest gave Henry a bad feeling.

"Do you remember the stories Alex told us, about the Lost Composer?" he asked. "He said that sometimes people left their belongings at the hotel. But when they called to ask the hotel manager to check the lost and found, their things were never found."

"Do you think the Lost Composer from the ghost story is a thief, and this is where they kept all the things they stole?" Jessie asked.

"Or maybe they found the items after the guests left and never brought them to the lost and found," Henry suggested. "They kept them for themselves."

"Whoever wants the keys returned to Room 222 needs them to open this chest," Violet guessed. "They know what's in the chest, and they're willing to ruin Juliette's party to get it!"

"So all we have to do is find out who knows about this chest," Jessie finished.

Henry nodded. "Let's lock the chest back up and go tell Juliette."

Violet used the key to lock the chest and gave the key back to Henry, who put it in his pocket. Benny pulled the tarps over the chest so it looked the way it had when they first found it.

Jessie opened the door to the shed, and they left quietly. It was getting very dark now, and she was eager to get back to the hotel.

There were two exits from the clearing going back into the hedge maze.

"Does anyone remember the way back through the maze?" Henry asked.

"I do," Violet said, pointing at the left exit. "That way. I'm sure of it!"

Just as they were about to head back through the maze, Benny caught Jessie's hand. They all paused. Jingling was coming from the other direction!

"Someone saw us go into the shed!" Benny said.

"It's probably the person who left the message about the keys," Henry said. "Maybe they led us out here to see if we'd unlock the chest. If we can catch up with them, we'll know who's trying to cause all this trouble for Juliette!"

Henry peered over the top of the hedge maze. It was hard to see in the dark, but he thought he saw someone creeping through the hedges.

"I don't know," Jessie said. She checked her watch. "It's getting late, and it's really dark. What if we get lost in the maze?"

Henry nodded. Jessie had a good point. They had an important decision to make. And they had to make it soon, because the jingling sound was growing quieter. Whoever was making it was getting away!

TO FOLLOW THE JINGLING, GO TO PAGE 91.

TO GO BACK TO THE HOTEL, GO TO PAGE 98.

THE JINGLE

"Let's get to the bottom of this, once and for all!" Henry said.

The jingling trailed off down the hedge path that went away from the hotel. The Aldens hurried after it. They were sure to stay together so they didn't get separated in the thick, dark maze. Benny had a good ear. He followed the jingling through the dark, and the others followed him deeper into the labyrinth.

"It sounds like keys!" Benny said.

"If the Lost Composer was really a person who was stealing people's things and putting them in a secret chest, it would make sense if they had a set of keys!" Jessie agreed.

Benny took a left, then a right, then another left

through the hedges. All the hedge paths started to look the same, but Benny's sharp ear kept them on the trail of the jingling noise. The noise grew louder and louder. They had almost caught up to it!

"This way!" called Benny.

They turned a sharp corner around a prickly hedge and as they did, they saw a small, dark shape scampering away up ahead. They ran after it, taking turn after turn through the maze until finally they reached a dead end. Even Henry was a little out of breath from their dash through the maze.

"Oh—that's the Lost Composer?" Violet said, out of breath.

Crouched at the end of the hedge path was a big cat with long, black fur. The moonlight reflected in its big yellow eyes.

"It's just a cat!" Benny said. "The same one we saw in the mirror!"

Violet walked up to the cat carefully so she didn't scare it. At first the cat seemed nervous, poofing its tail and arching its back.

"It's okay," Violet said. "We didn't mean to scare you. We thought you were a thief!"

The cat's tail smoothed when it heard the gentleness in Violet's voice. It walked up to her and meowed. She knelt and held out her hand. The cat came up to her to be pet. As Violet scratched around its neck, its collar jingled. There was a little bell attached.

"To think, all this time we were chasing a cat!" Jessie exclaimed.

"But whose cat is it?" Benny asked. "Juliette said no cats were allowed in the hotel!"

Violet inspected the cat's collar. In addition to the little bell that was making the noise, it had a name tag. "That cat's name is Clara," she said. "It says she belongs to an E. G."

"Eddie Gardner," Henry said. "I haven't forgotten how grumpy he seemed about Juliette not allowing cats, and how you saw his duffel bag move. He must have snuck his cat into the hotel even though it was against the rules. Then Benny saw it in the two-way mirror because he was keeping it in the secret room. He must have been planning to use the cat and the other things he knew about the hotel to scare the guests!"

"But why would he do that?" Jessie asked. "The hotel belonged to Eddie's family. If it became a landmark, it would be honored and remembered, even if it doesn't belong to the Gardner family anymore."

"Also, why does he want the keys to the treasure chest?" Benny asked.

"I don't know," Henry said. "But right now, all the signs point to Eddie Gardner. We should get back to the hotel and tell Juliette what we've learned. It's almost midnight."

As the four Alden children turned to head back through the maze, the cat leaped from Violet's arms. A moment later it disappeared under the hedge, like a shadow in the night. The jingling of its collar faded away.

"I hope it went back to the hotel," Violet said. The sky had grown so dark it was almost black. "I want to go back to the hotel too."

"Do you remember the way?" Jessie asked Violet.

"I'm not sure. I remembered the way to the shed, but then we started chasing the cat and I lost track," Violet said.

"Let's try to retrace our steps," Henry suggested. They followed him as he headed down the hedge corridor. "I think it's a right, here...no, wait, maybe a left?"

They turned left. Then right. Then left again. A few minutes later, they ended up in a dead end.

"Is this the same dead end where we found the cat?" Benny asked.

"I'm not sure...let's try again," Jessie said.

Left. Right. Left again. But this time they were in the middle of three pathways.

"It doesn't make any sense," Henry said. "I'm totally lost!"

They tried again and again. Henry tried to see over the top of the hedges, but in the dark it was impossible to make out the shape of the maze. The mansion's lights shone over the hedges, but no matter how they tried to reach the old hotel, they always ran into a prickly, dense hedge.

Eventually they ended up in another dead end.

"I think we're going in circles," Jessie said. They sat down to catch their breaths. From the hotel, they could hear the distant voices of guests. Henry checked his watch.

"It's already 11:57," he said. "I don't think we'll make it in time."

He was right. A few minutes later, they heard the distant sound of a pipe organ playing, followed by the frightened cries of the guests. The grand opening party was over early, as the guests rushed out. The Lost Composer had struck again.

THE END

TO FOLLOW A DIFFERENT PATH, GO TO PAGE 90.

RETURN TO THE HOTEL

"I think we'd better get back inside," Henry said. "It's so dark, and if we get lost in this maze, we're not going to be able to help anyone solve the mystery. The jingling will have to wait."

Violet led the way back through the hedge maze. She had a good memory and was confident she knew how to get back to the hotel. The others followed. The jingling faded.

"Benny's right. It really did sound like keys," Henry said as they followed Violet.

"If the Lost Composer were stealing people's things and putting them in a secret chest, it would make sense if they had a set of keys," Jessie agreed.

Violet stopped and held a hand out.

"Shh," she whispered, holding a finger to her

lips. "I think someone's in the maze with us!"

They all lowered their voices and listened. They could hear the sounds of footsteps shuffling somewhere in the maze. It was getting closer! The Aldens crouched and held their breaths as the footsteps came right up on the other side of the hedge.

"Clara," said a voice in a low hiss. "Clara!"

Jessie turned to Henry and silently mouthed, "Who's Clara?"

Henry shrugged.

The voice whispered the name a few more times then grumbled. The footsteps stomped off into the maze.

"Whoever that was is headed toward the exit," Violet said.

"Do you think it was the person who was watching us by the shed?" Benny asked. "The person who wants the keys to the treasure chest?"

"I don't know. I didn't hear any jingling," Jessie said. "Let's go."

Violet nodded and looked left, then right. She remembered this place!

"This way!" she said, and she turned right. After

a few twists and turns, the hedge maze opened, and they could see the main garden against the side of the hotel.

"We're free!" said Benny.

Someone else was heading from the garden to the hotel. In the dark, it was hard to make out his face, but it was definitely a young man.

"That's the person who was calling for Clara," Violet said.

"I think it's Eddie Gardner!" said Henry.

They followed the man back to the main entrance of the hotel. The lampposts on the front driveway and the warm light coming from inside the lobby was welcoming, especially after being in a maze in the dark. Hotel guests were talking on the steps and in the lobby. It seemed like everything was going well, at least for now. It wasn't midnight yet!

"It is Eddie," Jessie said when the light fell on the man's face. He glanced back. When he noticed they were following him, he scowled and hurried inside.

"Look at his shoes," Violet said. Eddie's shoes had spots of gray mud on them. The mud was the same gray color as the mud she and Henry had seen in the basement.

"Yeah, but look at ours," Benny said.

Their shoes were muddy too. It was from walking in the hedge maze.

"I wonder what he was doing out there," Jessie said. "Besides calling for Clara, whoever that is. Do you think he was spying on us, to see if we had the mystery keys?"

"Now is our chance to find out," Henry said. "If we talk to him, we can tell him we know it was him in the secret room. Then he might admit to being the one who followed us into the maze...and being the one who wrote that letter to Juliette."

"But what about Clara?" Jessie asked.

"And we didn't hear the jingling sound when we saw him in the maze," Violet added.

Benny sighed. "Every time we learn something new, I just think of new questions! My head's spinning!" he said.

"You're right," Henry said. "It doesn't all add up. But we've got to make a decision soon. It's almost midnight!"

IF THE ALDENS CONFRONT EDDIE GARDNER,
GO TO PAGE 103.

IF THE ALDENS PAUSE TO WRITE OUT WHAT
THEY KNOW, GO TO PAGE 111.

CONFRONTING MR. GARDNER

The Aldens hurried through the lobby after Eddie.

"There you children are!" a voice called. The voice belonged to Juliette. She came out of the crowd just as Eddie Gardner disappeared in the other direction. "What's going on? It's almost midnight. Have you figured out who sent that message?"

"We're pretty sure it was Eddie Gardner," Henry said. He nodded in the direction Eddie had gone. "He just ran that way."

"It's almost midnight," Violet said. "He must be on his way to do whatever he's been planning if he doesn't get the keys!"

"Not if we stop him," Juliette said. "All right. Let's go talk to him together. I'd love to put an end to this ghost nonsense once and for all."

The Aldens went with Juliette as she followed Eddie. The lobby was so crowded with guests that he hadn't been able to get very far. They caught up with him just as he headed up the grand staircase toward the second floor.

"Eddie!" Juliette called. "Wait a minute. I'd like to speak with you."

Eddie paused when he heard Juliette.

"Sorry, I don't have time right now. I've lost something, and I need to get back to my room," he said.

They joined him on the second-floor landing, where they could speak without being overheard by the guests. Eddie scowled, looking back and forth between the Aldens and Juliette.

"What's this about?" he asked.

"We know you were just in the hedge maze," Henry said.

Eddie's eyes went wide.

"I—I was in the hedge maze, yes, but what's wrong with that? It's part of the grounds. I was just trying to get some fresh air!"

"And we're pretty sure you were in the secret

room connected to Room 222, as well," Jessie continued.

"We also know about the treasure chest in the garden shed," said Benny. "We're not going to give you the keys, and we're not going to let you ruin the grand opening either!"

Eddie shook his head, confused.

"Wait—what keys are you talking about? There's a treasure chest in the garden shed? I don't know what you mean."

"The message!" Juliette said. "You don't remember what you wrote? 'Bring my keys to Room 222, or I won't rest until everyone is gone.' I'd think you of all people would want your father's building recognized by the historical committee."

Eddie frowned deeply.

"I admit it—I did something I shouldn't have. I...I snuck my father's cat, Clara, into the hotel."

"Clara is a cat?" Jessie asked. "Is she black, with long fur?"

"Yes, have you seen her? She also has a little bell on her collar. I heard her out in the maze, so I went after her."

"The cat I saw in the mirror!" Benny said.

"Yes. My father named her after Clara Schumann, a famous composer. I got her after my father passed away. She lived in the hotel as a kitten, so I thought tonight it would be nice to visit when it reopened. But then I found out Juliette changed the rules so pets weren't allowed. I was keeping her in Room 222, but when she heard you in the hallway, she jumped and escaped out the window. And I went into the secret room."

Eddie ran his hand over his forehead, worried.

"I've spent all evening trying to find her," he said. "I'm really worried. But I didn't leave any creepy note, and I don't know anything about mysterious keys or a chest in the shed. I promise."

"There's a secret room in the hotel?" asked Juliette.

The children had forgotten to mention that to Juliette. "Yes, you can open a door to it by knocking one of the books on the shelf in Room 222," Violet said.

"And the food elevator goes all the way up there!" Benny added.

"He means the dumbwaiter," Jessie explained. "Eddie, did you go down the dumbwaiter tonight when we found the secret room?"

Eddie sighed and nodded. "The room was my father's private study," he said. "The truth is, I came here tonight to try to find out why my father lost the hotel. I wasn't very close with him, but the building has been in our family for a long time. I just couldn't understand why it had closed. So when I heard someone else had bought it and was reopening it, I came to meet you and try to learn more about what happened before my father passed away."

Juliette sighed. "Eddie, you could have asked. The hotel failed because of all the ghost stories and bad reviews. Guests couldn't sleep because they said they heard the organ in the lobby playing all night. When their items went missing and the hotel manager couldn't find anything in the lost and found, your father was accused of stealing."

"I didn't know any of that..." Eddie trailed off, tilting his head. Then he let out a big sigh. "Oh no. I wonder if the organ was my father playing late at night. Do you remember that keyboard in his study? It controls the organ in the lobby."

Benny gasped. "So it wasn't the Lost Composer at all!"

"The Lost Composer?" exclaimed Eddie. "Is that the name of a ghost?"

"Yes! The Lost Composer scared guests and stole items," Violet said. "At least, those are the rumors. Now we know that the organ playing was just your father practicing late at night."

"But what about the missing items?" Jessie asked.

Eddie shook his head. "My father would never steal from guests. I didn't know him very well, but I know he wasn't a thief."

"I'm getting worried," Juliette said. "If Eddie isn't the one who wrote the message about the keys, then who was? It's almost—"

Before Juliette could finish, the clock in the lobby rang. It was midnight. The guests who were enjoying the party quieted to listen to the clock tolling the time. But when the last chime tolled, the lights began to flicker.

"Oh no," Juliette said.

"What's happening?" Eddie asked.

All the lamps and ceiling lights went on and off, and the guests started to murmur. Suddenly gusts of steam burst out of the radiators, filling the lobby with a hazy glow. Finally the lights shut off altogether. The lobby was completely dark.

Organ music started to play loudly.

The guests started to panic. Someone screamed with fright.

But Eddie noticed something. "The music isn't even coming from the organ," he said. "It looks like it's coming from that old-fashioned record player over there. Someone must have just switched off the power to the lights and turned on the power to that record player!"

"We've got to stop them," Henry said. "They're scaring the guests!"

It was too late. Guests were hurrying out of the dark lobby. Without any lights on, and with the panic caused by the organ music, it was hard to get anyone's attention. Grandfather found the children on the stairs.

"What's going on?" he called.

Juliette had given up trying to call the guests back inside. She watched the last four guests, the historical committee, leave. They didn't look scared of the organ playing or the radiators blowing steam. They didn't even seem afraid of the dark. Still, from their faces, it was clear they weren't impressed.

"You should get your electric box and boiler fixed," said one of the women. "This could be a safety hazard."

"It's very unprofessional to have these kind of issues during opening night," said another.

Juliette sighed and sat down on the stairs.

"So much for the historical landmark registry," she said.

THE END

TO FOLLOW A DIFFERENT PATH, GO TO PAGE 102.

LISTING THE FACTS

"Let's not jump to any conclusions," Jessie said. "I think it'll be smarter if we write down everything we know. Some things still don't make sense. We wouldn't want to accuse someone if we're not sure they did something wrong."

"Good idea, Jessie," Henry said. "Do you have your notebook?"

"I left it with our things in Juliette's office," said Jessie. "Let's go there where it's quiet. But we should hurry. It's going to be midnight soon!"

The four children walked calmly through the lobby. Guests chatted and ate fancy snacks. The children even passed Alex and Anita, who had changed into fancy clothes and were pouring sparkling drinks into polished crystal glasses.

When they got to Juliette's office, they shut the door so it was just the four of them. It was nice to have some quiet to focus on their task. Jessie took out her notebook.

"All right, let's see. What do we know so far?" she asked.

"Whoever wrote the note to Juliette wants the keys to the treasure chest in the shed," Benny said. "And they're going to pretend to be a ghost and scare everyone if Juliette doesn't do what they want!"

"And the chest is full of things that are probably stolen," Violet added. "Stolen by the ghost known as the Lost Composer."

Jessie nodded and wrote down the things that Benny and Violet said.

"The keys to the chest were on the old key ring Juliette had when she took over the hotel," Henry said. "She didn't know what the keys went to. But this means that whoever wants the keys knows about the chest and what was in it, and also knows about the hotel from before Juliette took over."

"Right," Jessie said. "That rules out everybody who works here today."

"What about the secret room, the mirror, and the cat?" Benny asked.

"I think Eddie Gardner brought a cat into the hotel," Violet said. "He was mad about the no-pets rule, and we saw his duffel bag move. Since we know now that the cat you saw in the mirror wasn't a ghost and was actually a real cat, my guess is that he brought a cat to the hotel and is hiding it in that secret room."

"Eddie's father did own the hotel," Henry agreed. "If anyone knew about the secret room above Room 222, it would be him. And if he brought a cat and had to hide it somewhere, that would be a good place."

"Do you think he brought the cat to scare people?" Benny asked.

Jessie sighed. "He might have, and he might know about the chest in the garden shed too. But what I don't understand is why he would want to ruin the night. The building belonged to his family. Even if he wanted the keys to the chest, why would he risk scaring away the historical committee when they're visiting?"

"He must have been doing something else in the maze," Benny said. "He was calling for Clara. If he wanted to spy on us, he wouldn't have been making all that noise."

The four of them read the notes Jessie had taken.

"Who else might know about the chest and the keys, and also be willing to scare away the historical committee?" Henry asked.

"We forgot to write down some other clues," Violet said. "Henry, remember the mud we saw in the boiler room, and the wrench? Like someone was doing something to the boiler?"

"Yes," said Henry. "We saw the same mud on the maintenance man's boots."

"And then we all got muddy going in the hedge maze," Benny said.

Henry nodded. "Yes, but all that means is that Sebastian was probably out in the maze too. And that he may have gone down to the boiler room. The mud down there was wet, so whoever tracked it in had done it recently. When we met Eddie this afternoon, he didn't have any mud on his shoes."

"Why would Sebastian do this?" Violet asked.

"He lost his job when the hotel was closed," Jessie said. "And I suppose being a maintenance man, it would be easy to get in and out of guest rooms. If Sebastian were the Lost Composer from the ghost stories and stole all those things, he could be trying to get them out of that locked chest."

"It was a lot of money," said Benny. "But do you think Eddie could be the Lost Composer?"

"Hmmm." Henry thought about that and what they knew about Eddie. "Since the hotel belonged to his father and he probably knows about the building's secrets, it's possible he could use that to scare people and get into their rooms. But that was also a long time ago. He would have been very young, maybe Benny's age."

"Woooooo!" Benny said, waving his hands. "I'm the Lost Composer! Woooo!"

They laughed. It was a funny to imagine Benny as a ghost.

Henry, Jessie, Violet, and Benny reviewed Jessie's notes.

"Well, we have two suspects," Henry said. "Eddie Gardner and Sebastian, the maintenance man. It's almost midnight, so we need to make a decision and tell Juliette before the clock strikes twelve. What do you think?"

IF THE ALDENS CONFRONT EDDIE GARDNER, GO TO PAGE 103.

IF THE ALDENS CONFRONT SEBASTIAN THE MAINTENANCE MAN, GO TO PAGE 117.

CONFRONTING THE MAINTENANCE MAN

The Aldens hurried back to the lobby.

"There goes Eddie," Violet said. They looked to the grand staircase, where Eddie was hurrying up to the second floor. He looked upset, wringing his hands as if he were very worried.

"Let's tell Juliette we think Sebastian is behind the message," Henry said.

They found Juliette chatting with Grandfather near the grand staircase. She was fidgeting with her necklace and sighed with relief when she saw the children.

"Did you figure out who left the message?" she asked. "It's so close to midnight. I'm getting worried."

"We think we know who we need to find," Henry

said. "Have you seen Sebastian?"

"Sebastian?" Juliette repeated. "Yes, actually. I saw him a little while ago. He said something was broken in the boiler room and asked if he could fix it for old time's sake. Why? Are you saying you think he's the one who's trying to scare off the guests?"

"Yes. We found a locked chest of stolen items out in the garden," Jessie said. "The keys open the lock. We think Sebastian is the Lost Composer, and the chest is where he was keeping all the items he was stealing from guests."

"And now he's pretending to be a ghost so he can scare everyone away—unless you give him those keys!" said Benny.

"Hmph! Well, he's not going to be getting the keys. And he's not going to scare my guests away or ruin this party either!" Juliette said, putting her hands on her hips. "Let's go down to the boiler room and see what he's up to. James, would you keep an eye on things up here?"

Grandfather nodded. He wasn't worried at all.

"Of course, Juliette. Good work, children. I knew you'd be able to help Juliette tonight, but I didn't know you'd get to solve such an exciting mystery!"

The Aldens and Juliette made their way through the crowded lobby, down the hall, and to the door that led down into the basement. Juliette unlocked the door and went in first, flipping the light switch at the top of the stairs.

"Sebastian?" she called. "Are you down there?"

No one replied, but Benny's ears perked.

"I hear jangling!" he said.

When Henry and Violet had first come down into the musty, old basement, it had seemed pretty dark and creepy. But now that Juliette was there it seemed just like a normal part of the building. She went down the stairs first.

Heat and white steam were oozing from the boiler room. It was hazy like something out of a scary movie, but Juliette just waved the steam away.

"Sebastian. Is that you?" she called.

They heard more jangling coming from the boiler room. The sound echoed against the bare walls. They also heard high-pitched hissing and clanging. Juliette walked right up to the door and pushed it open.

"I thought we'd find you here," she said.

Sebastian the maintenance man was stooped over the boiler, holding a wrench. Steam was coming out of some of the pipes, but he wasn't trying to fix it. In fact, he was unscrewing one of the valves!

"Juliette!" Sebastian said.

"Stop that right now," Juliette ordered. "Give me the wrench."

Juliette was good at giving orders, and even Sebastian did what she said. He stepped away from the boiler.

"His belt!" Benny said.

On Sebastian's belt was a ring of keys. As he moved, the keys clinked against each other and made a jangling noise.

Juliette took the wrench from Sebastian and handed it to Henry.

"Henry, tighten the nuts on those pipes before they pour steam into the whole hotel," she said. "Sebastian, what were you thinking? Is it true you wrote that message?"

Sebastian frowned.

"I—I'm sorry," he said. "Yes, I wrote the message. But if you would have just given me the keys, then I wouldn't have had to do this."

"You didn't have to do it either way," Violet said.

"Now that I don't have a job, I needed the extra money and I thought if I could get the things from the chest, I would be able to get by!" Sebastian said.

Juliette sighed. "Sebastian, this is all wrong. One of the reasons I wanted the committee to approve the hotel was because if it became a historical landmark, we'd be busy enough that I'd be able to rehire you. But now I'm not sure, knowing that you were stealing from hotel guests!"

"No, please! I didn't steal the items," Sebastian said.

"You didn't sneak into people's rooms and take things?" Henry asked.

Sebastian shook his head. "No. I'd only find them after people left. Sometimes I'd find them weeks later."

"Then why did guests report hearing a jangling noise on the nights their possessions went missing?" Juliette asked. "I've heard the ghost stories, same as everyone else. Your keys jangle, and you knew about all the missing items. And why would a maintenance man walk around the halls in the middle of the night?"

Sebastian sighed. "Nighttime was when Mr. Gardner—Eddie's father—was awake. And he barely ever left his study. He even had his food delivered to him on the dumbwaiter. Night was the only time I could talk to him, so I was always going up and down the secret hallway and staircase. As time went on, he cared less and less about the hotel, so I had to catch him when he was awake and talk to him about all the maintenance that needed to be done."

"What do you mean, cared less and less?" Jessie asked.

"I don't think he ever really wanted to run the hotel," Sebastian said with a shrug. "He only did it because it belonged to his family. He was much happier when he was composing. The older he got, the less he took care of the building...and his employees."

"And that's when you started pocketing the

items people left behind," Juliette said, putting her hands on her hips. "Those things didn't go missing because of a ghost. But Mr. Gardner wasn't paying enough attention, so you were able to take them for yourself."

"But you weren't expecting to have the keys to the secret chest in the shed taken away," Henry finished. He finished retightening all of the boiler equipment Sebastian had loosened. The steam stopped pouring out of the pipes, and the eerie hissing noises stopped. "So you came up with a plan to get the keys back so you could get to all the items you took."

Sebastian hung his head.

"I'm sorry. I was worried about making ends meet. I shouldn't have tried to do it by threatening to scare the guests away," he said.

"Well, the good news is, you didn't," Juliette said. "Come on, everyone. Let's go upstairs."

The four Aldens, Juliette, and Sebastian went up the stairs and down the hall into the lobby. The guests were all having a great time. There were no ghosts to be seen! Grandfather saw them return and gave them a little salute.

"Looks like everything worked out!" he said.

Violet nodded, although she still had leftover questions.

"What are you thinking, Violet?" Henry asked.

"I still have some questions," she said. "Like Eddie's bag and the black shape we saw in the secret room. We even heard a jingling in the maze, but I don't think it was Sebastian, since he was in the boiler room that whole time. And Benny and Jessie saw a cat in that two-way mirror!"

BING-BONG.

The clock struck midnight. The guests listened to the chimes as they echoed through the lobby. Even Sebastian was quiet, watching the clock with a peaceful look in his eyes.

"What's that?" someone asked, pointing.

The curtains near one of the windows rippled, even though there was no wind. A jingling noise came from behind the curtains. But this jingling wasn't the sound of a ghost's keys in the middle of the night. It was the jingling of a little bell.

"Oh no!" cried one of the guests. "A jingling

ghost! The rumors are true!"

Suddenly, a black, shadowy shape shot out from behind the curtains. It darted behind a couch, then under a chair, then right between Grandfather's ankles!

"That was a pretty small ghost!" said Grandfather.

Violet laughed. She knew better.

"It's not a ghost!" she said. "It's a cat! Come on. I think we're about to answer my leftover questions!"

CONTINUE TO PAGE 127

THE LOST COMPOSER LIVES ON

The Aldens left Juliette and Grandfather in the lobby and followed the quick black shape down the hallway. Even though it was black and easy to lose sight of in the dim hall, the jingling noise was never very far ahead. Finally they turned a corner and saw the creature clearly for the first time.

"Oh, it's so cute!" said Jessie.

It was a big, black, fluffy cat with a collar. On the collar was a little bell. When the cat stopped to give itself a good scratch behind the ear, the collar made a familiar jingling sound.

"That's the cat I saw in the mirror!" Benny said.

"Hello there, little one," Violet said. "Did you get spooked by all the people in the hotel? I bet you're looking for your owner!"

Violet went up to the cat carefully, kneeling down. When she held out her hand, the cat came toward her, and she pet it gently on the back. Next to the bell on the cat's collar was a silver name tag.

"It says her name is Clara," Violet said. "And that her owner is E. G."

"Eddie Gardner," Henry said. "So this is who he was calling for out in the hedge maze."

Someone's footsteps echoed down the hall. Around the corner came Eddie. He looked worried, and then gasped with relief when he saw Clara the cat.

"There you are!" he called. "I've been so worried about you!"

Clara ran up to Eddie and jumped into his arms and began purring. A moment later Juliette came to see what was going on.

"I thought I said no cats were allowed, Eddie," Juliette said. Although she didn't really sound angry.

"I'm sorry!" Eddie said. "She is very good at sneaking around this old hotel. In and out of rooms like a shadow...But still I thought I'd be able to keep an eye on her. I only brought her with me to the hotel because I thought she might like to visit. She grew up here when she was a kitten. But then you said there was a no-pets policy, and—"

"So you snuck into Room 222 and the secret study to hide her?" Benny asked.

"Secret study?" Juliette asked. "What secret study?"

Eddie shook his head and let out a big sigh.

"I was going to tell you, but I didn't because I was mad about the pet rule. Now I guess you ought to know. My father had a secret study."

"You can get to it through Room 222," Jessie said. "By knocking the book on the bookshelf."

"Knocking the..." Juliette's voice trailed off.

Eddie nodded. "Yep. Knock, knock, knock—"

"The knocking guests used to hear in the middle of the night!" Juliette exclaimed. "And what do you mean by his music? I didn't know Charles Gardner was a musician."

"Maybe Charles Gardner wasn't," Eddie said with a smile. He stroked Clara between the ears. "But Charles Ivy was."

"Charles Ivy, the famous composer?" Juliette asked. "You're telling me..."

"Say, Juliette. Is the historical committee still here?" Henry asked.

"Yes. They're back in the lobby, I think," said Juliette.

The Aldens exchanged glances. Then Henry looked at Eddie.

"I think I know a way to make this evening end on a great note," he said. "Follow me."

***

Everyone followed Henry into the lobby, where they saw the group of four well-dressed members of the historical committee. Henry told his siblings, Juliette, and Eddie to wait while he went to get them.

"Excuse me," he said as he approached the historical committee. "My name is Henry Alden. I was helping Juliette Baker with the grand reopening tonight. She let me know that you were the historical committee and were considering the hotel for the historical landmark registry. Is that correct?"

"Yes," said one of the men. "The building is quite magnificent. However, there are many other mansions like it in the area. I'm afraid it doesn't set itself apart enough to become a landmark on the registry."

"I was hoping we might see some ghosts," said one of the women jokingly.

"Well, that's why I've come to speak with you," Henry said. "During the course of the night, I've learned something that might interest you. It may change your mind about the building."

Henry gave a big smile.

"Interesting!" said one of the men. "Yes, indeed. I am curious."

Henry waved them to the grand staircase where his siblings, Juliette, and Eddie were waiting. From the snack bar, he saw Grandfather raise his eyebrows, impressed.

Henry introduced the historical committee to his friends.

"This is Juliette, whom you've already met," he said. "And this is Eddie Gardner, the son of the previous owner."

"Nice to meet you," Eddie said.

"Eddie, the historical committee is looking for something to set the hotel apart from other buildings like it," Henry said. He raised his eyebrows, giving Eddie a signal. "I think you know something about it that might interest them...and even a place in the building that could prove it. Don't you?"

Eddie's face brightened as he understood what Henry was talking about. He nodded with excitement.

"Yes!" he said. "Yes, in fact, I do. Please, would you follow me?"

The small group went up the grand staircase, and Eddie led the way down the hall to Room 222. When they got into the room he put Clara down, and she scampered to the warm spot in front of the fireplace. The historical committee looked around the room. They didn't seem impressed until Eddie pulled the book out of the bookshelf.

Knock, knock, knock! The secret door opened, and the members of the committee gasped with delight. Juliette lit up when she heard the knocking and stood next to Eddie.

"Did you hear that famous knocking?" she said. "Those knocks inspired dozens of ghost stories that have been told for years. But no one knew the real reason for the knocks—until now."

Eddie held out his hand and gave a little bow. "Please, follow me."

For the first time, Henry saw excitement in the eyes of the historical committee members. Chatting between themselves, they followed Eddie down the secret hallway. They marveled at the two-way mirror, but when they reached the music room at the top of the stairs, they went silent in wonder.

One of the women noticed the music sheets lying in stacks on the desk and music stands. "Charles Ivy?" she asked. "These are handwritten notes. Are you telling me that Charles Ivy—"

"Is the late Charles Gardner," Juliette finished. "Eddie's father."

One of the historical committee members inspected the keyboard, then followed the cables that came out of the back of it. "This keyboard. It must be connected to that marvelous organ in the lobby, is that right?"

"Yes. This is where he composed some of his most famous and favorite works," Eddie agreed with a wide smile. A jingling noise came from the stairs as Clara came to join them. She jumped into Eddie's arms, and he gave her a kiss on the head. "Apparently became the inspiration for some famous ghost stories too."

"Astounding!" said the historical committee leader. "Well, I can't be more impressed. Although the building is in fine shape, I thought before this there was nothing to set it apart. But knowing that not only have you done a wonderful job restoring it, but that it's also the place where the great Charles Ivy wrote his music—why, there's no doubt in my mind now that it should be added to the national registry."

Juliette practically fainted. "That would be amazing. A dream come true," she said. She turned to the Aldens and then to Eddie. "And with all the new business that's sure to come, I'll be able to rehire Sebastian too. Thank you so much—this

night has been truly grand."

"We were happy to help," said Jessie.

"I'm just glad everything worked out," Henry added.

"And that there weren't actually any ghosts!" Benny said. "By the way...did you say the keyboard goes down to the organ in the lobby?"

"Yes," Eddie said. "Whatever you play here will come out of the organ downstairs."

Benny looked at the keyboard excitedly.

"Do you think I could...?" he asked. "Just this once...?"

Juliette chuckled and motioned toward the keyboard.

"I'm sure Eddie's father would love it if you did the honor," she said.

Benny hopped up and down with excitement and sat down at the keyboard. The historical committee gathered around, interested in how the old keyboard would work. As Benny played a single chord on the black and white keys, they could all hear the organ playing in the lobby below.

Someone downstairs cried out in surprise,

and Benny stopped playing before he frightened anyone else. Still, he couldn't keep the big smile from his face. If only for a moment, the ghost of the Lost Composer had lived again.

THE END

TO FOLLOW A DIFFERENT PATH, GO TO PAGE 116.

Meet the Boxcar Children

HENRY ALDEN

At age fourteen, Henry is the oldest of the Alden kids. He likes to figure out how things work, which makes him good at repairing and building stuff! While he'll never brag, he's a great runner too! It's not always easy being the oldest and having so much responsibility, but there's nothing that Henry can't handle.

JESSIE ALDEN

Jessie is twelve and a natural leader. She's very organized—she makes lists in her notebook and always keeps track of facts when there's a mystery to be solved. When her younger siblings need help, Jessie's there. She loves planning adventures and taking care of Watch.

VIOLET ALDEN

Everyone knows ten-year-old Violet is creative—she loves to draw, take photos, and play the violin. She's a little on the shy side, but because she's quiet, she's a careful observer. With her artist's eye, Violet picks up on important details that her brothers and sister sometimes overlook.

BENNY ALDEN

Benny's only six, but just because he's the youngest Alden, it doesn't mean he can't help solve mysteries. He's always curious and full of questions. In fact, one of his favorite questions is "When's lunch?" because he's usually hungry! Benny loves playing with Watch and visiting new places.

WATCH

Watch is the family dog, a friendly and smart wire fox terrier. When the children lived in the boxcar in the woods, they found him as a stray. Since then, he has been loyal to the Aldens, especially Jessie, who once removed a thorn from his paw. Watch also has a special bond with Benny, who gives him treats!

Visit www.boxcarchildren.com/meet-the-boxcar-children to take the Boxcar Personality Quiz and find out which character is most like you!

Add to Your
Boxcar Children Collection!

The first twelve books are now available in
three individual boxed sets!

978-0-8075-0854-1 · US $24.99   978-0-8075-0857-2 · US $24.99   978-0-8075-0840-4 · US $24.99

The Boxcar Children Bookshelf includes the first twelve
books, a bookmark with complete title checklist,
and a poster with activities.

978-0-8075-0855-8 · US $69.99

The Boxcar Children 20-Book Set includes Gertrude
Chandler Warner's original nineteen books,
plus an all-new activity book, stickers,
and a magnifying glass!

978-0-8075-0847-3 · US $132.81

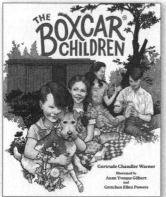

This fully illustrated edition
celebrates Gertrude Chandler
Warner's timeless story. Featuring
all-new full-color artwork as well as
an afterword about the author, the
history of the book, and the Boxcar
Children legacy, this volume will be
treasured by first-time readers
and longtime fans alike.

978-0-8075-0925-8 · US $34.99

THE BOXCAR CHILDREN ® GREAT ADVENTURE

An Exciting 5-Book Miniseries

**Henry, Jessie, Violet, and Benny Alden
are on a secret mission that takes
them around the world!**

When Violet finds a turtle statue that nobody's seen
before in an old trunk at home, the children are on the
case! The clue turns out to be an invitation to the
Reddimus Society, a secret guild dedicated to returning
lost treasures to where they belong.

Now the Aldens must take the statue and six mysterious
boxes across the country to deliver them safely—and keep
them out of the hands of the Reddimus Society's enemies.
It's just the beginning of
the Boxcar Children's
most amazing
adventure yet!

JOURNEY ON A
RUNAWAY TRAIN
Created by Gertrude Chandler Warner

HC 978-0-8075-0695-0
PB 978-0-8075-0696-7

THE CLUE IN THE
PAPYRUS SCROLL
Created by Gertrude Chandler Warner

HC 978-0-8075-0698-1
PB 978-0-8075-0699-8

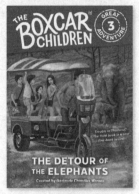

THE DETOUR OF
THE ELEPHANTS
Created by Gertrude Chandler Warner

HC 978-0-8075-0684-4
PB 978-0-8075-0685-1

THE SHACKLETON
SABOTAGE
Created by Gertrude Chandler Warner

HC 978-0-8075-0687-5
PB 978-0-8075-0688-2

THE KHIPU AND
THE FINAL KEY
Created by Gertrude Chandler Warner

HC 978-0-8075-0681-3
PB 978-0-8075-0682-0

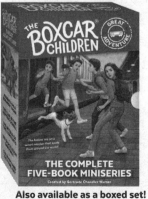

THE COMPLETE
FIVE-BOOK MINISERIES
Created by Gertrude Chandler Warner

Also available as a boxed set!
978-0-8075-0693-6 · $34.95

Hardcover US $12.99 · Paperback US $6.99

Don't miss the next two books in the classic Boxcar Children series!

THE BOXCAR CHILDREN®

BOOK 148

CREATED BY GERTRUDE CHANDLER WARNER

Something is roaming the hills under the full moon...

THE LEGEND OF THE HOWLING WEREWOLF

HC 978-0-8075-0740-7 · US $12.99
PB 978-0-8075-0741-4 · US $6.99

HC 978-0-8075-0737-7 · US $12.99
PB 978-0-8075-0738-4 · US $6.99

Introducing The Boxcar Children Early Readers!

Adapted from the beloved chapter books, these new early readers allow kids to begin reading with the stories that started it all.

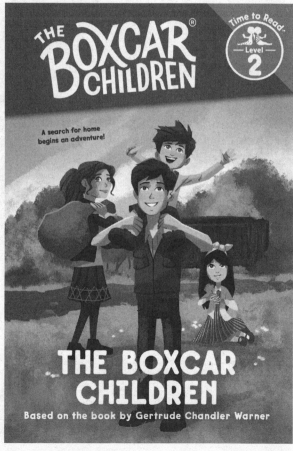

978-0-8075-0839-8 · US $12.99

Look for *The Yellow House Mystery* and *Mystery Ranch*, coming Spring 2019!

978-0-8075-7675-5 · US $12.99

Look for the new animated movie, *Surprise Island*, coming August 2018!

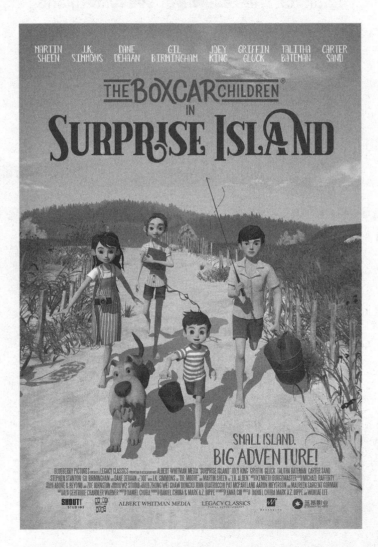

NEW!
The Boxcar Children
DVD and Book Set!

This set includes Gertrude Chandler Warner's classic chapter book in paperback as well as the animated movie adaptation featuring Martin Sheen, J.K. Simmons, Joey King, Jadon Sand, Mackenzie Foy, and Zachary Gordon.

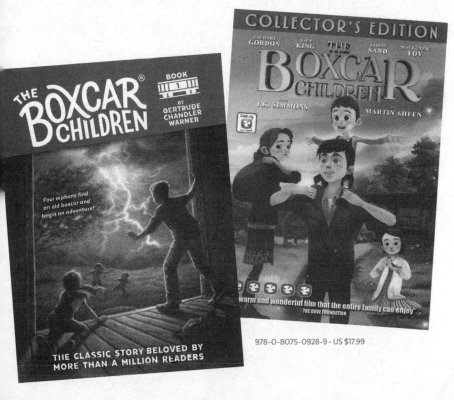

978-0-8075-0928-9 · US $17.99

GERTRUDE CHANDLER WARNER discovered when she was teaching that many readers who like an exciting story could find no books that were both easy and fun to read. She decided to try to meet this need, and her first book, *The Boxcar Children*, quickly proved she had succeeded.

Miss Warner drew on her own experiences to write the mystery. As a child she spent hours watching trains go by on the tracks opposite her family home. She often dreamed about what it would be like to set up housekeeping in a caboose or freight car—the situation the Alden children find themselves in.

While the mystery element is central to each of Miss Warner's books, she never thought of them as strictly juvenile mysteries. She liked to stress the Aldens' independence and resourcefulness and their solid New England devotion to using up and making do. The Aldens go about most of their adventures with as little adult supervision as possible— something else that delights young readers.

Miss Warner lived in Putnam, Connecticut, until her death in 1979. During her lifetime, she received hundreds of letters from girls and boys telling her how much they liked her books.